the event

the event

Juan José Saer

Translated by Helen Lane

Library of Congress Catalog Card Number: 94-68598

A complete catalogue record for this book can be obtained from the British
Library on request

First published in Spanish as *La Ocasión* in 1988 by
Ediciones Destino S.A., Barcelona

This edition first published in 1995 by
Serpent's Tail, 4 Blackstock Mews, London N4
and 401 West Broadway #1, New York, NY 10012

Set in 11pt Garamond
Printed in Finland by Werner Söderström Oy

For Laure and Philippe Bataillon

Let us call him simply Bianco. The fact that at certain periods of his life he went by the name of Burton, he will explain one day to Garay López, was due merely to the color of his hair, since he was of the opinion that being called Bianco might ruin the credibility of a redhead. A. Bianco perhaps, as he often signs his name firmly and carefully, with a laborious and complex flourish, aimed more toward identification than toward aesthetics. A. Bianco, an echo of what in other periods of his life has also been A., but standing for Andrew, A. Burton, and which, after the run-in with the positivists in Paris, he decided to change. Andrea Bianco perhaps? A. Bianco, in any event, to be sure, although the initial, instead of shedding a bit of light on the mystery, on the contrary makes it more obscure, so that since he prefers it, and even though that name conflicts with his obscure origins and with the color of his hair, which even at the age of forty-six is a thick shock of reddish curls, we are going to call him, to simplify things, just Bianco.

As it happens, he is now standing, hesitantly, in the middle of the pampas, and because of the gray, unvarying air, not too cold, of this afternoon at the end of winter, his carroty hair, his reddish eyebrows and eyelashes, verging on brick-colored, seem even redder still; some two hundred meters behind him, the cabin, the only rudimentary elevation on the flat and monotonous surface of the ground covered with gray grass, constitutes a precarious, somewhat inconsequential background, more of a stage set than a dwelling, whose modesty contrasts with the expensive attire, obviously European, of its owner – the owner not only of the cabin but of the entire pampas that extends from his feet to the horizon and which would once more extend from his feet to the horizon if he were standing at another point of the circle which, by an optical illusion, joins the gray sky to the plain. This is the rear of the cabin, a rectangular adobe wall of a grayish brown, topped by the inclined plane of one of the two slopes of the thatched roof. Seen from a distance, it does not look as though it were any thicker than a painted backdrop, for Bianco has insisted, when he had it built by one of Garay López's day laborers, an old half-breed of mixed Spanish and Indian blood, who specialized in such things, that he wanted it to be as simple, as austere as possible, just big enough to contain a cot, a little table, a lantern and a cupboard, only what was strictly necessary to spend a few days, every so often, far from the city, in complete solitude, so as to devote himself entirely to thinking, in order to refute once and for all the arguments of the positivist cabal that, six years earlier, had forced him, in one way or another, to leave Europe. But now that he has come outdoors, his mind elsewhere, to see whether the gray sky is going to bring rain and decide whether he will go back to the city that very evening or the following morning, struck, as often happens to him, by a practical idea in the midst of his philosophical reflections, he has started thinking about bricks, so that for the space of a few brief moments the images that unfold, swiftly but clearly behind his forehead, have the same reddish color as his thick shock of hair, rising in rather stiff waves that cover over these images on the outer surface of his head.

When, six years earlier, he had seen the pampas for the first time, near Buenos Aires, in the week following his arrival, it had appeared to him almost immediately, that because of its silent and deserted monotony, it was a place that favored reflection, not for the rough and resistant thoughts, of the same color as his hair, like those that he is now having, but for the smooth, colorless ones above all, those fitting together in unalterable and transparent structures, which ought to serve him to liberate human space from the servitude of matter. The flat expanse, with no surface irregularities, that surrounds him, as gray as the sky at the end of August, represents better than any other place the uniform emptiness, the space devoid of the phosphorescence of ill-assorted colors that the senses emit, that translucent no man's land inside his head where strict, silent and clear syllogisms concatenate. But he does not scorn other thoughts either, whatever their color, brick-red for example, such as now, or those thoughts that tint Gina's matte skin and become curved, as round as the contours of her body, as black and sleek as her hair, as abrupt and as slightly childish as her laughter, as supple and humid as her surrender of herself. His contempt for material things comes perhaps from the ease with which he understands them, resolves them, masters them. Thus, on arriving on the pampas with the title deeds to his property, he decided at a single glance, observing the rich landowners round about, that he too would devote his efforts to cattle raising and to commerce – to do everything that rich people do if one wants to become rich, became, once he was able to frequent them and study them from close up, his golden rule; thanks to his astuteness, to his sense of practicality, which in his case is a gift as is in others the aptitude for music, that practical sense now colors his thoughts the same shade of brick-red as his hair, for he knows that immigrants are arriving by dozens, by hundreds of thousands on this plain where, for leagues and leagues around, there is not a tree or a stone to be seen, and these immigrants, when they have made a little money growing wheat and want to live in more substantial houses than the huts made of dung and

straw that they build when they first arrive, will need bricks
which he, Bianco, will manufacture and sell to them.

Banishing these thoughts with severity, with disdain almost,
in unvoiced contention with himself, since he knows that his
pragmatic projects sometimes have the nature of a puerile, and
above all inefficacious, revenge against what has banished him,
Bianco walks on a little farther, making the gray grass crackle
beneath his European boots, and concentrates his attention on
the plain. The echo of his footsteps lingers in his memory, as
clearly as at the moment when they trampled the grass, a totally
unquestionable and well-defined acoustic apparition, with perfect contours within the limitless hollow silence, like objects in
space and even, on this plain, closer to the senses and to memory
than objects. For a few seconds Bianco gets lost in the gray
transparency of the exterior, obviously present and clear
although inconceivable, each detail of which – a black bird that
slowly crosses the sky high above, the uniform layer of gray
clouds, the gray expanse of the grass, the cold air that brings a
little color to his cheeks, the overwhelming evidence of his body
– is like a rending or a danger, a mass or a sharp edge of the
material magma that poisons him, the petrified lava in which
the positivists want to bury the species, whereas he, Bianco, has
already demonstrated several times that thought governs matter,
models it as it pleases, traverses it and shifts it around, and that,
filtering through the bones of the skull, as water does through
porous walls, it rediscovers, by itself, thought beyond the bones
and the organs; that it suffices to concentrate, to work on and to
refine these gifts in order to get the better of the repugnant iner-
tia of matter and show, by transgressing its supposedly
ineluctable laws, its nature as a secondary formation, of a minor
effect of a plan that holds it in contempt or ignores it, as an
excremental residue of the mind. All of Europe has had to bow
before the evidence that he, Bianco, has presented to it for

nearly ten years – he thinks at this moment, with a somewhat humiliated indignation, shaking his head, a prey to a powerless conviction that exasperates him and makes him exclaim aloud, in Italian:

"Science has several times verified my gifts!"

Giving a start at the sound of his own voice, he looks around him, feeling somewhat embarrassed, fearing that someone might have caught him talking to himself in the desert, even though he knows that there is no other human being anywhere around for several leagues, except for the overseer and the four cowhands looking after the herd of cattle, to whom, moreover, he has given orders to stay away, insofar as possible, from the cabin that serves him as a retreat, and he is obliged to recognize, which makes his humiliation even worse, that what has caused his start of surprise is the fact that, despite the six years that have gone by, the wound continues to bleed to the point of making him lose his equanimity and to oblige him, in the cold winter afternoon, to gesticulate at and argue aloud with nothing but the pampas. He can read the thoughts of others, move objects at a distance by concentrating mentally, modify the shape and even the intimate substance of metals by merely touching them; in London, Maxwell himself, who shortly thereafter was to unify the electromagnetic field, was present at one of his experiments, personally verifying the conditions under which it was conducted and was obliged to bow before the irrefutable facts. So that it is not worth the trouble to lose control of himself. It is true that after the positivist ambush in Paris his gifts were impaired, and that for several years, upset by the campaign that French journalists were waging against him, he abstained from these practices, but for several months and thanks to the collaboration of Gina, in whom he is practically certain that he has perceived the signs of the necessary gift, he has begun once again to work on his concentration and his faculties of telepathic communication.

Without managing to convince himself completely, Bianco allows his thoughts to calm him down and ventures a little farther away from the cabin. The fleeting, slightly painful, vision of the adverse matter that is imprisoning him, once again becomes the empty, bare pampas, the flatland of which, for six years, he has been the sole owner and where the cattle that he let loose on it when he took it over keep endlessly multiplying, passive, at his disposal and docile. Just as easily as his sense of practicality has allowed him to detect with the greatest of ease the possibilities of making money – by attentively observing, wherever he went, the rich people of the place and acting precisely as they did, with the supplementary advantage of doing consciously what in their case was a mere instinct of self-preservation – his basic pragmatism has allowed him to adapt to the almost obligatory barbarism of the pampas and to act in it with such perfect spontaneity that the gauchos in his hire whose wages he pays punctually and with a certain generosity, base themselves less on his somewhat ostentatious propriety than on the quite visible revolver he wears at his waist, so as to make himself a reputation which, in the region, impels prowlers, even the most dangerous ones, to stay a long way away from the austere cabin where he comes to meditate. "Congratulations my dear friend," Dr. Garay López is in the habit of saying to him with a slightly derisive admiration: "You have obtained in only a few years, and by nothing but a unilateral decision, what my family, who are descendants of the founder of the city and already have had four governors among its members, took three centuries to obtain by theft and the whiplash." In his particular manner of conversing with him, mingling together Spanish, French, English and Italian phrases accompanied by elegant and ironic gestures, just a touch histrionic perhaps, Garay López often reminds him of this fact, expressing in admiring terms a fundamental disapproval that Bianco tolerates since he is well aware that if it were genuine, Garay López would not be his partner in the business of importing wire fencing from Germany to resell it to the cattle raisers of the province.

Stopping short, Bianco lifts his head. The birds, five or six of them which at present are crossing the sky, are making their way, unlike the flock that he has seen a moment earlier, on swift wings, more or less helter-skelter, as though something had frightened them; therefore, instinctively, Bianco lowers his head once again and begins to scrutinize the horizon in the direction from which they are coming, and it seems to him that he sees, at the very point where the earth and the sky join, a minuscule spot, flattened and moving, like irregular and nervous strokes made with a pencil so as to clumsily efface a horizontal line. Intrigued, he stands stockstill, observing the mobile scribbling which, standing out a bit on the horizon, disturbs its smooth emptiness. Well-rounded but solid, not so much enveloped in fat as thickset or stocky, beardless, preoccupied, or rather, self-absorbed, with a bitter droop to his lips, even in the era of his European glory, with his leather jacket over his Scottish woolen shirt, his wine-colored corduroy trousers tucked into his high-topped boots, his reddish hair and eyelashes and the bluish veins that slither beneath the furrows of his brow and around his eyes, he gives, for several seconds, the impression of being not a human being but the statue representing him, a reproduction in wood, coated with rather clashing colors, a recently painted anachronism erected in the middle of the pampas.

It was in London, fifteen years earlier, around 1855, that he became a figure of renown. At that time, he went by the name of Burton, A. Burton, and he claimed to have been born in Malta, explaining in this fashion his Italianized English, unpolished and rudimentary. But later, on the continent, he will permanently adopt the name of Bianco so as to escape the legendary mistrust of Europeans vis-à-vis the English and thereby facilitate his introduction into intellectual and scientific milieus. The island of Malta, with its prestige as a center of esotericism and its mixed tradition, at once Oriental and Occidental, allowed him to reinforce his aura and, paradoxically, to increase, by blurring his precise origins, his credibility. It was only later, after the positivist conspiracy, that, determined to leave Europe, he will work for the government of Argentina in exchange for property rights, inducing Italian peasants to come settle on the pampas, that he will adopt Italian nationality and make Tuscan his mother tongue, somewhat atypical perhaps, in view of the years he has spent in Prussia, in England, and in France, and of his mania, his superstition almost, for persisting in speaking all languages, not, moreover, without a certain facility, but with a foreign accent difficult to identify and that sometimes gave the impression of a malformation of the tongue that impedes correct speech. Because of these uncertainties of diverse sorts – natal, racial, linguistic – Garay López, to show that he is aware of them but that he has decided, as befits a true gentleman, to ignore them, hails him in several languages at once: "Cher ami ... dear friend ... caro amico!", strongly accenting the last word and looking him straight in the eye with a smile full of veiled complicity, which irritates Bianco and even sends him into a fury, especially since he is obliged to pretend that he hasn't noticed the allusion.

In London, around 1855, he emerged from the shadows, in a second-rate theater, to exercise his powers, telepathic thought, movement of objects at a distance, distortion of matter through simple contact, and to maintain that this gift, which he himself had mastered to perfection by practicing it for years, is within the power of everyone and that all one need do is to believe in it and to dissolve that excremental residue of the mind constituted by matter, as he takes pleasure in calling it, in order to exercise it fully, with the result that the theaters in which he performed were filled to overflowing by people who brought their spoons, their iron bars, their old vest pocket watches with broken springs and who, concentrating under his direction, gripped them in their hands with all their strength, with their eyes closed, convinced of the secondary nature of agglomerated substances, until the metal bars or the spoons twisted or broke to pieces, as though they had been made of soft caramel or clay, and until the watches began to keep time again. As the theaters became more central and more spacious, the scientific authorities to whom Bianco appealed publicly to verify his demonstrations became stricter, and his main tactic, paying a call on the skeptics who insulted him in the newspapers in order to propose to them, with no restrictions whatsoever, the supervision of the controls imposed upon him, managed to win his detractors over. Maxwell himself in the end asserted to a reporter: "Mr. Burton and I are doubtless working in a similar experimental field that it would be difficult to define within the framework of a mere interview; we differ only as to our method, our hypotheses and our objectives."

Another of his gifts was telepathy. He invited to the theater those psychiatrists who raised objections, had them draw in secret on a sheet of paper in one corner of the stage and then reproduced the design before the public, in colored chalk on a large blackboard, more or less precisely but almost always in a form very much like that of the original, which was then spread out so as to compare it with the reproduction drawn on the blackboard; and Bianco, gravely and without an excess of self-pride, maintained that, unlike the difference of matter and its capricious and asymmetrical forms, mind does not manifest itself except in certain great universal figures that reproduce, contain and explain the essence of all things, and that all that was necessary was to know how to perceive them and decipher them: "All that is required is patience and sincerity," he would say. "We" – onstage he used the royal "we" – "seek neither to engage in polemics with materialists or to convince them. We are not unaware of matter, nor do we deny it. We merely wish to demonstrate its secondary nature."

Two years later, the doors of the university were thrown open to him – not only the lecture halls but also the physics laboratory and the medical and psychiatric amphitheaters. One day, at the end of one of his demonstrations, a sickly-looking young man, prematurely bald and noticeably timid, introduced himself to him, saying that he was the son of a high Prussian dignitary and that he wished, in the name of the authorities of his country, to invite him to give a series of lectures, but before that event took place, he would be delighted to invite him to have lunch in London. Unlike what his rachitic air would leave one to suppose, the young Prussian ate with gusto and engaged in energetic and frank conversation; not only did he agree that Burton, in order to demonstrate his gifts on the continent, should change his name and begin to be known as Bianco, but even strongly recommended that he do so; the young man's advice was followed, not in one fell swoop but gradually, so that during his first year in Prussia Bianco went by both names, sometimes one, sometimes the other, and even in certain cases the two of them at the same time, until he had adopted, exclusively, Bianco, saying Burton had been the name of his mother; the fact is that, at heart, he felt an uncertainty about his name, a resistance at letting himself be represented by a sole patronymic, as though he was afraid that, by choosing too definite a name, a number of parts of his being would dry up and disappear.

For six or seven years still, he continued to proclaim Malta as his native island, there where Templars, Gnostics and Saracens had lived side by side or whose paths had at least crossed and intensified its aura, archaic and ill-defined, with their obscure flashes of light.

For several years, Prussia welcomed him and fêted him – he frequented the nobility, scientific circles, actresses and members of the general staff of the Army. From time to time, the embassies organized lectures abroad for him, demonstrations at universities, meetings with scientific authorities and even with religious authorities who saw in his theories concerning the supremacy of the mind an unexpected and modern confirmation of old dogmas from which the masses were beginning to disassociate themselves. Paris wrought its magic on him, and on his return to Prussia, he began, having become a little weary of provincial life, to prepare for his departure so as to make Paris his permanent residence and send out from there his message to the entire world. But he feared that his Prussian protectors would not allow him to leave. To his surprise, they greeted the idea with enthusiasm and soon invited him to present himself to the general staff for a private interview with one of its principal officers. The officer received him affably, offered him a cigar and explained to him the reason for their interview: the intelligence service would like Herr Bianco, thanks to his gifts for telepathy, to undertake to fathom the secrets of the French general staff, in an indirect way, naturally, profiting from his eventual friendships in Paris and his frequentations of milieus that the Prussian Embassy would take charge of gaining him entry into. "Malta, colonel, is my native island," Bianco replied, "and England the scene of my first scientific demonstrations, but Prussia is my adopted homeland and the country imposes duties that gratitude and honor preclude my evading."

And so he settled in Paris. Academic and scientific milieus, skeptical less out of intimate conviction than out of professional interests, looked upon him with reticence, but from salon to salon, from grand gala to grand gala, from adultery to adultery, he finally won the indispensable relationships, and at the end of a year, he was a notable whom a handful of adepts considered to be the living proof of the sordid unreality of matter, while a swarm of snobs competed for his attention at well-attended lunches and elegant afternoon chocolate parties. The newspapers engaged in controversy concerning his case; a member of the Institute attacked him, but the Academy of Sciences, more prudent, defended him, arguing that *a priori* attacks scarcely accorded with the experimental method and that the century authorized its impartial application to any object whatsoever, wherefore it, the Academy, did not pronounce itself either for or against as long as the necessary tests had not been carried out. In his public demonstrations, now less frequent, Bianco continued to twist little coffee spoons and metal bars, to make unusable watches work again, to reproduce almost to perfection, through thought transmission, designs hidden from his sight, which, after a moment of painful concentration, he drew in colored chalk on a blackboard; his mere proximity made compass needles waver with uncertainty, made magnets capricious, caused screws to move like insects. Go back home, concentrate, forget the prestige of matter, he would say, and its stubborn resistance will vanish once you have subjected it to the continual fire of the mind, of whose superior power I am the living proof. And the watches started ticking again; the metal bars twisted; compass needles spun about wildly.

Every so often, he would draw up a report for the Prussian Embassy, without great conviction, awaiting the moment to free himself of his mission, for he regarded it as unworthy of his gifts and dangerous for his reputation; but when he hinted at that possibility to the officials at the embassy, these civil servants gave him to understand that this possibility was extremely remote, for from the moment that he had drafted the first report his fate had been linked to that of the general staff until the end of time. Bianco approved with a resigned smile that accentuated even more the bitter expression of his mouth without there being any way of knowing whether it should be attributed to the very shape of his lips or to a grimace acquired in the course of the obscure first thirty years of his life.

One day, the Academy of Sciences sent him a letter proposing that he perform a demonstration in their laboratories. The time had come, the letter said, for him to prove his gifts for telepathy and telekinetics before a select group of scientists, without the presence of the general public and in experimental conditions that the Academy itself would establish. The Academy's basic premise was that both sides would act in good faith and it thought that a meticulous experiment could not help but be useful to science. Bianco did not fail to note the peremptory and slightly stern tone of the letter but the challenge excited him, even though he suspected a trap and accepted knowing that if he triumphantly proved his point, what he called in salons and theaters his simple truth would thereby be regarded as possessing an invincible and definitive nature. On a winter afternoon, he went off, alone, to the Academy and subjected himself to the proposed experiment. Eight persons supervised it; among them, a middle-aged man, dressed in black, who kept looking at him sympathetically. As dusk fell, they let Bianco go, but did not announce their decision as to the results. In the street, the middle-aged man caught up with him, looked him over for a moment with a curiosity full of admiration and invited him to dinner.

According to him, the members of the Academy appeared to be convinced of the genuineness of his gifts and the conclusions would no doubt soon be made public in the form of a communication that would be made by one of the scientists present who would thus assume the role of spokesman. He for his part was entirely convinced, but he was only an attorney and a journalist. He thought that, in order to put pressure on the Academy to announce its decision in short order, Bianco ought to hold a great public demonstration in a theater, and if Bianco agreed, he, the attorney-journalist, would take charge of organizing it. Bianco reflected in silence for several minutes, warming his glass of cognac in the cupped palm of his hand, and finally accepted.

The journalist did a fine job: he filled the largest theater in Paris with disciples and detractors, with journalists, scientists, artists, bureaucrats and members of the military. He had also organized, in addition to the usual experiments, a debate during the intermission so that Bianco might explain the origin of his work and his supporters and his enemies might freely put forth their arguments, but on ascending to the stage, Bianco felt that the evening was going to be stormy, and that to judge from the shouts and constant disputes in the audience, the number of skeptics was infinitely superior to that of the believers. He began to speak none the less: he was by no means a scientist but merely a humble object who placed himself at its disposal; in his youth, he himself had had doubts as to his powers, immersed as he was, because of the education that he had received, in the excremental magma of matter, which in this century was an object of worship; he himself had suffered from the same skepticism displayed by many of those who were in the audience, having for many long years been assailed by doubt and gone astray, refusing to believe in his own gifts, which existed, he was certain, in each and every one of the persons present in that theater, in whom they had simply atrophied through lack of use. During his speech, he was obliged to put up with shouts, guffaws and one or two interruptions but his supporters, and even certain of his detractors, raised their voices to demand silence, in firm and solemn tones. Finally, a number of scientists insisted that he proceed to perform the experiments. Bianco maintained that the audience was too agitated for him to be able to obtain the concentration necessary, but knowing that if he backed down, his simple truth, as he called it, risked being shattered to bits, he began his demonstration in a precarious silence and the spiteful attention of the audience, twisting, by the simple imposition of his hands, the well-known iron bars and spoons, making small metal objects change place on a transparent table, making broken watches that had been rusting away for years work again, causing compass needles to go wild and reproducing, by mental concentration, on a blackboard with bits of colored chalk, the design that someone had made at the other end of the stage, out of his sight, on a sheet of paper that he then carefully folded in four. When he had finished his demonstration, the shouts and the catcalls drowned out the applause until one of the scientists managed, with great effort, to silence the audience once more so as to address a brief speech to those present: "We are going to perform a comparative examination between Monsieur Bianco's demonstration and that of one of the eminent members of the Institute (*laughter*) who has been kind enough to offer to participate in our experiment." And, holding his arm out toward the wings just as an orchestra hidden in the pit abruptly began to play circus music, he invited someone waiting behind the scene to come onstage.

A clown, his face hidden behind a mask and a huge red nose, made his appearance, pretending to run as fast as he could as meanwhile he advanced very slowly until he had reached the middle of the stage, and without uttering a word, keeping time to the music that grew slower and slower, he began to perform, with great rapidity and facility, all of Bianco's experiments, twisting iron bars, starting watches going again, making compass needles abruptly change direction, moving every which way, receiving objects from a group of scientists on his right and then passing them on, in a different state, to those on his left, and little by little, there was created, beneath Bianco's thunderstruck gaze, a sort of round, the scientists on the right receiving from the audience spoons, pieces of iron, watches and compasses and passing them to the clown who started the watches again, twisted the pieces of iron and then passed them on to the scientists on the left, who examined them and then handed them back to the audience. "I'm a prestidigitator! I'm a prestidigitator!" the clown began to shout: "I'm a prestidigitator but I'm also a positivist!" The audience was in an uproar and there began to rain down onstage, in Bianco's direction, spoons, watches, iron bars, compasses. Bianco tried to fling himself on the clown but those onstage held him back as the clown now began to produce, from out of nowhere, doves, bouquets of flowers, a rabbit, silk ribbons, colored paper streamers that floated about onstage, and kept shouting without a letup: "I'm a positivist! I'm a positivist! I'm a positivist!" with inordinate fury, almost in a sort of trance, until, turning around, he approached Bianco and murmured to him: "I've been through all that myself, my esteemed colleague. Twenty years ago, I had the same temptation and in my case too, it turned out badly." And as he took off his mask and his fake nose, Bianco recognized the journalist, his companion, whose absence, a while earlier, had deeply disturbed him, for his eyes had searched in vain for him onstage and in the audience as he was carrying out his demonstration.

The following day, the news appeared in all the papers. Since one of them insinuated that Bianco was probably, apart from being an impostor and a mythomane, a spy in the service of one of the traditional enemies of the nation, not only were the doors of salons closed to him but also those of the embassy which, in the face of repeated insinuations, found itself obliged to publish a communiqué in which it was explained in detail that the person in question had hurriedly left Prussia some years previously after having been found guilty several times of abuse of confidence and of fraud. After retiring for a time to Normandy to a house which overlooked the Seine, Bianco, who, two times out of three, ran across, even in the countryside, someone who recognized him (his picture often appeared in the newspapers or in magazines, both before and after the scandal), decided that it was perhaps necessary to go back for a while to the obscure, hazy area from which he had emerged when he was about thirty, and gathering together all his worldly goods which, despite the reverses of fortune, were not negligible, since his practical sense and his prudence in financial matters were in no way contaminated by his excesses and his predilection for risk in other areas, he boarded a ship at Le Havre and went to settle in Sicily.

He had a good job but rancor gnawed at his heart. In the beginning, even in Sicily, he seemed to detect, in certain gazes that met his in the street, a mocking allusion to past humiliations. One day, he reprimanded, in his Italian made rigid by that strange accent in which he spoke every language, a man who stared at him for a longer time than was courteous perhaps, only to perceive afterwards that the person in question hadn't even seen him and that his absent gaze was simply focused on a vague point in space as he listened to a music box that he was holding in his hand. Another time, he left a restaurant in a fury because it seemed to him that a group of people who were speaking in loud voices and laughing at a nearby table were making fun of him. For several months, he suffered from this sort of hallucinatory attack. One evening, in a brothel in Palermo, he slapped a whore because she was French and had laughingly asked him if he was acquainted with Paris. But finally he calmed down, or rather entered into a sarcastic half-sleep, accompanied by a certain gluttony and a slightly ostentatious reactive alcoholism, which the waiters of the most luxurious restaurants in Sicily regarded with condescension. It was as if, by eating and drinking, he were trying to bury himself in his own body as though in a cave in which he need only lower the trap door over his head like a tombstone. But that phase didn't last either; his body was unable to bear it. After a month in bed, because of a sort of rheumatism, of generalized pain, terrible but difficult to locate at any precise point in his body, he began to calm down and to tell himself that after all, if he went out for a stroll with his cane, his best clothes, his hat, on the seaside promenade and if he happened to come face to face with anyone who had been present at that spectacle that night in Paris, he would have no reason to fly into a temper, for if the addicts of the secondary, of the residual conglomerations that go to make up matter, had won a skirmish, he could take his revenge by writing; an evening in the theater cannot help but be destroyed by time, whereas a written text, a summary of thoughts linked one to the other and placed one beneath the other on a sheet of white paper and then multiplied by printing, was something indestructible. He needed to lose himself in the shadow again for several years and then emerge with these luminous pages.

A chance meeting furthered his plans. One day, in a hotel in Agrigento, he made the acquaintance of an Argentine diplomat, a consul or something of the sort, who was traveling all over Italy in order to persuade poor peasants to come settle on the pampas on lands that the Argentine government would furnish them. In all truth, the consul was more interested in Magna Grecia than in agriculture, and after several days spent visiting ruins and eating their meals together in the hotel restaurant, the consul told him that if it would interest him to become a representative of the Argentine government, he could offer him in exchange the property rights to twenty square leagues of good land for growing crops and raising cattle in the northwest of the pampas which the government was aiming at populating. All he would have to do would be simply to convince the greatest possible number of Italian peasants and send them off by boat to Argentina. Six months later, with his title deeds in his valise, on a boat recklessly overloaded with emigrants, Bianco, leaning on the rail of the upper deck, his brick-colored hair a bit ruffled by the wind, gazed with interest but without emotion at the virtually nonexistent port of Buenos Aires.

The earth, level with the water, without relief, without a single cliff, merging with the enormous brown river that was a prolongation of the sea, the deserted seacoast, the group of insignificant dwellings and, on the lower decks, the immigrants, crowded together around their bundles of rags, contemplating as though spellbound the edge of the unknown, trying to guess what there might be on the other side of it, with the hope of finding there what he, Bianco, on coming to seek them out in the fields of Piedmont, of Sicily or of Calabria, had promised them in order to persuade them to board a crowded ship, in third class and even in the holds, fore and aft, while he, Bianco, traveled on the upper deck, in a cabin specially fitted out for him, adjoining that of the captain, with whom he had played cards during the entire crossing and whom he had amused, in the course of their nights of drunken revelry, with magic tricks performed with only his left hand since his right hand was immobilized by an enormous abscess on his ring finger that got worse during the crossing. The abscess, caused by an ingrown nail, formed on the end of his finger a blister of pus that had burst several times and then formed again, each time even bigger than before, and seeming to him, secretly, to be the point where his body was concentrating the last vestiges of past humiliations, the final expulsion of those sediments of corrupted and deceptive matter which, like a poison, had been coursing in his blood lately, so that, leaning on the ship's rail, he averted his gaze from the exciting desert that awaited him, twenty square leagues of which were already his property, and fixed his eyes instead on his swollen red ring finger, deformed by a large border of pus around the nail, with a faint trace of that bitter smile that one found it impossible to say whether it was etched in the very configuration of his lips or whether it was a mark, like a scar, that dated back to his obscure years.

Standing motionless in the middle of the pampas, Bianco scrutinizes the horizon. The slight, moving scrawl, which altered the line where the sky joins the gray earth, has become a skittish, elongated spot, which little by little takes on relief above the horizontal line and which, as it becomes detached from it and comes closer, disintegrates and is transformed into an infinity of points and then in dark spots which tumble about and which, progressively, grow larger, raising a distant rumble that has not yet reached Bianco's ears but which the birds, the moles, the hares, the partridges and the weasels of the pampas have already perceived, and agitated by it, are beginning to flee in all directions. A hare passes, hugging the ground, leaping in the air in terror to skirt the tall tufts of dry, sparse grass. Two partridges come out from the bushes and, flying low, sluggishly cover a short space then plunge back into the underbrush and take flight again a little farther on. Flocks of birds in the sky disperse on swift wings. A mole knocks against the wall of its burrow, then stands stockstill. At present the louder and louder rumble mounting from the horizon begins to reach Bianco's ear and little by little, just as the original spot has disintegrated into a proliferation of little dark spots, still without form, the dull rumble spreads out into an increasing, multiple noise which none the less maintains a certain uniformity and which Bianco deduces is being produced by the gallop of many horses. He pats his revolver at his waist and abruptly rousing himself from his immobility, heads at a run toward the cabin. As he turns the corner of the side wall and arrives at the front of the building, he very nearly stumbles over two tethered horses which have brought him from the city and will take him back again, and which are indifferently chewing, without appetite or conviction, tough blades of dry grass. Bianco enters the cabin, grabs a carbine from the table and goes back out into the open.

The herd is coming across the plain at full gallop, scattering and increasing in number as though by discontinuous changes in size, and beneath the horses' legs the sound of hoofs resounds and reverberates, spreading out into the air where birds are taking flight in every direction. Disregarding the fine rain that is beginning to fall and is spreading out, silently, over his face and hair, Bianco, reasoning that there are no horsemen riding these animals, lowers his carbine and stares, with an expression in which alarm gives way to surprise and then to astonishment, at the enormous dark herd approaching at full gallop, arousing the desert half asleep from the end of winter. There must be more than two thousand of them, more than two thousand, Bianco thinks, stirring a little in his excitement and repeatedly pounding on the ground, to calm himself, with the butt of his carbine. The horses, all with dark coats, their hair of an almost identical color, moving at the same rhythm, at the same speed, in the same direction, a somber, palpitating mass, a multitude unified by all its members and at the same time separate in each one of them, an agglomeration of warm flesh, muscles, nerves and senses, spreads, as it comes, its uproar throughout the empty countryside, so saturating it with its din that even Bianco's astonished thoughts are drowned out by the auditory proliferation and become, in his own mind, inaudible or incomprehensible to him. Vigorous, disciplined and wild, the horses resemble the archaic clay of being, shifting from place to place like a cosmic wind, divided into an indefinite number of identical individuals, like an infinity of stars separated by the darkness but all constituted of the same substance, or like a row of poplars sprung up from the same seeds, which, viewed from a certain point in space, are superimposed upon each other and intermingled to the point of giving the illusion of being but a single one. Or again, like discontinuous fine drops that fall from the sky and that, forming fine rain, make objects scattered in the gray void glow with dim and damp reflections. Bianco realizes that the ownerless herd traverses the pampas seeking green pastures in which to spend the winter, and he begins to run toward it with the preposterous plan of stopping it, of taking possession of it, of domesticating it, the deafening, unexpected gallop of the horses having brought him to such a point as to make him lose his sang-froid, that façade of calm and of unshakable decision that is already almost a legend for the others – Garay López, Gina, the ranch hands, those with whom he has commercial dealings, everybody – although in his inner-most heart, behind the mask to which his hair and his brick-red eyebrows lend an air at once strange and childlike, behind his bitter mouth, his trepidation is sometimes as intense as that produced by the horses' hoofs on the pampas. Indifferent to Bianco's running about in all directions, to his gesticulations, without changing either direction or speed, without stopping, without even noticing his presence, as though he and they were maneuvering in different times and spaces, the horses reach the point where he is standing and then begin to move off, still in a straight line, toward the opposite point of the horizon, and Bianco manages to continue to see the undulation of their dark croups gleaming from sweat or from the fine rain, as the din of their hoofbeats lessens and the horses themselves lose their sharp outlines in the silent water which becomes denser and denser, until the sound can no longer be heard and there remains only the dark spot, moving and anonymous, and when it finally is lost from sight over the horizon and disappears altogether, it reveals the insidious nature of its sudden fleeting and problem-atic apparition, rough-textured matter or vision, already so very nearly ungraspable by experience that its final passage toward the capricious and unverifiable manipulations of memory will merely lessen its pretensions to reality.

Still dazed by this apparition, Bianco, shaking his head slightly, realizes for the first time that a fine rain is falling, and starting to run, giving a little leap every so often to dodge a clump of grass higher than the others, he enters the cabin without even a glance at the two horses that give a slight start as they see him appear. With a rag hanging from one of the rafters, he wipes his face and his hair and after having quickly set the room in order again, putting two or three books back where they belong and placing a number of papers in a leather pouch, he wraps himself in a rainproof cape that reaches down to his ankles, slowly and carefully pulls his sombrero down over his head and goes out to saddle the horses.

"If everything goes well, I'll be with Gina by nightfall," he thinks, digging his heels into the horse that he is riding to make it trot. The animal docilely quickens its pace a bit, perhaps envying the relay horse which, free for the moment of all weight, trots at its side at a more relaxed, almost joyful pace. The man and the horses, surrounded by the heavy mist, although quite clearly outlined because of the damp gray reflections, none the less have something of the air of ghosts on the smooth, empty pampas, so perfectly identical to itself at every point that despite the horses' rapid gait, they seem to be enacting a parody of a cavalcade in the exact center of the same circular space. It is only the light that changes a little, imperceptibly and uniformly, penetrating the white particles of the fine rain, transforming them into a sort of ashen gray fog which, after an hour has gone by, abruptly turns a greenish color, a dark green like that at the bottom of an aquarium, then shading into a less and less transparent blue that grows denser around Bianco and the horses, and on the tufts of grass, so that finally it gives the impression that the horses, in their monotonous pantomime of a cavalcade, are splashing about in a puddle of ink. Before the

dark has swallowed everything up, Bianco, almost without reining in the horses, changes mounts, introducing a brief anomaly
into the rhythmic system that has been kept up for hours and
that, after this imperceptible hiatus, goes on in the same way
until Bianco and the horses become a little hazy at first, then
slightly darker and with vague contours, and finally invisible.

But with nightfall, they also reach the outskirts of the city,
the first houses, spread far apart and showing the lights of
kerosene lamps through the windows. Soaking wet, panting,
Bianco digs his heels, in vain, into his mount; intimidated by
the first obstacles, the trees, the houses, a few dark silhouettes
hurrying along in the fine rain, the animal trots reluctantly and
despite his haste and his fatigue, Bianco lets it do so, so that
they arrive in front of the house almost at a walk. As he climbs
down off the horse, Bianco notes the closed shutters, but notes
also that beams of light are filtering through the slats. After having quickly tied the reins to a post, making almost no noise, he
walks through the entry hall, his leather pouch in his hand and,
abruptly, opens the door to the living room.

Sitting in an armchair, her neck leaning against the back of it,
her head tilted slightly backward, her legs stretched out and
her heels resting on another armchair, her green satin slippers
fallen on the floor in disorder, Gina, her eyes half-closed, with
an expression of intense pleasure and yet, it seems to Bianco,
slightly equivocal, is taking a deep puff from a fat cigar that she
is holding between the index and the middle finger of her right
hand. Sitting in another armchair, a glass of cognac in his hand
and leaning slightly toward her, Garay López is talking to her
with a wicked smile and Bianco couldn't say whether Gina's
expression of pleasure comes from the cigar or from Garay
López's words, which she appears to be listening to, despite her
half-closed eyes, with a dreamy attentiveness.

For a second, Bianco stands there without moving, his right

hand on the door handle, his left holding the leather pouch, receiving on his wet face the first breath of the air of the room warmed by the fire on the hearth, feeling the muscles of his face relaxing a little so as not to give away the tumult roiling inside him and putting pressure on the reverse side of his mind, suspicion, hatred, despair, self-contempt, fury, discouragement and violence, but then, when he sees Gina leap out of her armchair, choking slightly on the smoke of the cigar and beginning to cough, and Garay López get to his feet and walk toward him with rather bewildered astonishment, Bianco recovers his self-control and with a calm, almost ponderous slowness, closes the door behind him and begins crossing the room.

"What a pleasant surprise, cher ami," Garay López says to him, shifting his glass of cognac to his left hand and offering him his right one, which Bianco grasps and shakes briefly in his, without prolonging his grip.

"Mine, I must admit, is less easily defined," Bianco says, and going over to Gina, who is still coughing, he gently removes the cigar from between her fingers and throws it into the fire.

Because of her fit of coughing, Gina has tears in her eyes.

"I wasn't expecting you until tomorrow," she says as she dries the tears away with the back of her hands.

"It's the rain that made me decide to come," Bianco says.

"There's nobody here, no cook, no maids, nobody," Gina says in a tone of voice that is at once a protest and an apology. "I'm going to go see what I can fix to eat. Will you stay, Antonio?"

Garay López hesitates, and before answering he looks at Bianco, without being able to hide a quizzical expression, hoping to find on Bianco's face a reply to Gina's rather abrupt question. But Bianco pretends not to have noticed. He too would like to scrutinize the faces of Gina and of Garay López in order to find out what images, what memories, what thoughts are throwing off sparks behind their foreheads, in the depths of eyes that betray nothing of what he would like to know and the suspicion of which makes him shudder, while at the same time he becomes suave again, though a bit stiff as well in his effort to appear natural and not give himself away either. But that demands an inordinate effort on his part, especially when he sees that Gina's pink dress, tight-fitting around the hips, is unbuttoned halfway down her bosom, and affords a glimpse of the woolen camisole that she wears in winter underneath her dress to protect herself from the cold without sacrificing her elegance, and also when he remembers that on opening the door and surprising her sitting in the armchair, her legs outstretched, in the act of puffing on her cigar, the hem of her dress was pulled up almost to her knees. Garay López's wicked smile, as he speaks to her in a low voice and provokes in her an expression of intense pleasure, has also cruelly incrusted itself in Bianco's memory, and hasn't stopped drifting about in it since the moment he entered the room. He intuits, moreover, that the visit has been a long one, for on a little table, near the armchairs, are two cups with an almost dry deposit of chocolate, remains of several different kinds of cake on a large dish and a number of cigar ends stubbed out in the ashtray.

Bianco pretends not to have heard Gina's question either and stands there waiting, without having come to any decision, without moving, without speaking, with his face and his hair that have been soaked from the misty rain and are now beginning to dry out in the heat of the fire, in such a way that the skin of his face draws a little and every so often he is aware of a slight movement in his hair which the rain has wet by way of the broad brim of his sombrero, every time that a shock of hair, flattened by the dampness, starts to curl again. Almost without realizing it, he would like Gina or Garay López to make some sort of move, but despite her question Gina stays where she is without budging, a little flustered and little by little recovering from Bianco's unexpected appearance, clearing her throat every so often and still coughing from the cigar smoke, as Garay López, after having sought for a few seconds, in vain, Bianco's acquiescence, drains the glass of cognac in one swallow, sets the glass down on the little table and begins to stroke, with a hesitant air, his recently trimmed black beard. "All this is taking too long. Say something," Bianco thinks, and, as though he hadn't heard Gina's invitation, proposes to Garay López, with constrained congeniality and a labored naturalness that clears a path for itself through his slightly hoarse voice:

"I won't hear of your leaving without having another cognac."

"Very well. But it's the last one," Garay López says, realizing that, in this way, Bianco thinks, the invitation to stay for dinner has been withdrawn, and the glass of cognac represents a compromise solution.

"Will you excuse me for a few minutes if I go dry myself off a little and change my clothes? I've been galloping in the rain since three o'clock this afternoon," Bianco says.

"And we were here, settled so comfortably. I'm filled with remorse," Garay López says.

"I'm going to the kitchen," Gina says. And to Garay López, without even shaking hands with him before she goes off: "Till tomorrow perhaps."

"No. I'm going back to Buenos Aires tomorrow. Everything is all arranged."

Gina turns toward Bianco.

"Shall I help you take your boots off? Do you need clean underwear?"

"I can manage by myself," Bianco says.

Gina looks at her green shoes flung on the floor, and sitting down in the armchair begins to put them back on. Between the three of them a tacit agreement appears to have been established, whereby it is understood that Bianco will not leave the room before Gina, and in the few seconds it takes her to put her satin slippers back on and head for the kitchen, Bianco and Garay López watch her in silence, admiring her and perhaps feeling a bit sorry for her, because of her extreme youth, or perhaps because of her being of the female sex, imagining her deprived of all her possessions, defenseless because of her beauty, in which there appears to be an element of unawareness, and the two of them doubtless a little wrought up by the raw evidence of her shapeliness that the pink dress, too close-fitting, emphasizes instead of concealing. When she disappears, closing the door behind her, a sensation, not totally extraneous to tears, to cruelty and to danger invade the room, amid the very slight creaking of the furniture and the waxed floor and the discreet roar of the flames on the hearth. Almost immediately, Bianco leaves the room, just in time to see, at the far end of the covered porch, the attenuated phosphorescence of her pink dress disappear in the half-shadow near the door of the kitchen. Crossing, beneath the drizzle, the patio of mosaic tiles around the cistern, Bianco reaches the porch on the opposite side and goes into the bedroom. There is no need for him to light the lamp to realize by the white patch that he begins to glimpse once his eyes become accustomed to the darkness, that the bed is unmade. He leaves his leather pouch in the semidarkness, and going out onto the porch, he takes off his sombrero and his cape, leaving them on a wicker chair and then, sitting down on the chair, panting a little from the effort, he takes off his boots and leaves them on the floor, alongside the chair legs. In his stocking feet, not making any noise, he goes back into the bedroom and lights the lamp. Heading for the washbasin, he hangs his jacket on the back of a chair, takes off his Scotch plaid shirt, his wine-colored trousers, his socks and his undershorts, and as he gets undressed, he does not cast a single glance at the completely unmade bed, the twisted sheets, the coverlet piled up at the foot, one of whose silk borders is touching the floor, the pillow folded in two and leaning against the headboard, and a large white cushion in the middle of the bed, with a slight hollow in it as though a body had been resting on top of it. Completely naked, his buttocks flat and white, his plump thorax thrust out and forming a single protuberance with his belly, quite flexible still, his legs, back and shoulders covered with freckles, his penis lost from sight between the sacs of his testicles hanging down amid a thicket of red hair, Bianco begins to pour water from the pitcher into the basin so as to wash himself, and only then does he dare to look at the bed, through the tilted mirror hanging above the washbasin which reflects it in its totality, as though this indirect way of observing it helped him to alleviate and to force the retreat of the multitude of abominable thoughts that, like ants from an anthill in flames, come out in terror and chaos from the darkness and begin to swarm in his awareness. He leaves the pitcher on the marble washbasin and goes over to the bed, sitting down, bare naked, on the edge. Because of the cold no doubt, or from some other unknown reason, the sparse, reddish hairs that cover the backs of his hands, his wrists, his forearms, begin to uncurl, to stand on end, and his skin breaks out in tiny bumps that make the diminutive craters of his pores swell, as he leans over toward the cushion, toward the sheet whose wrinkles the palm of his hand tries in vain to smooth out, and squinting, he examines the bed with care, with interest, with profound attention, feeling persistent pulses in the back of his neck and a painful rigidity in the muscles of his back.

"What a transformation, cher ami," Garay López says when he sees him come back into the living room, freshly washed and combed, in his house slippers, his Scotch plaid shirt different from the one he has just taken off, and his electric-blue corduroy pants, an ensemble as gaudy as the one he was wearing in the afternoon but in a different range of colors, as though some anomaly in his perception or in obscure areas of his personality required that chromatic surfeit in order to reach an equilibrium, unlike Garay López, whose elegance, which borders on dandyism, takes pleasure in the skillful and deliberately impoverished combination of three or four dull tones. Making an ambiguous gesture with his hand so as to conceal the importance of the supposed transformation, Bianco invites Garay López to sit down, not without observing that, during his absence, Gina has made a trip back to the living room, since the tray with the remains of the cakes, the cups of chocolate and the ashtray has disappeared. Bianco sits down facing Garay López, pours himself a glass of cognac without offering him any, and beginning to warm the drink in the palm of his hand cradled around the bottom of the glass whose stem he is holding between his middle and his ring finger, he leans against the chair back and looks at Garay López with a questioning gaze.

"I thought you were in Buenos Aires," he says.

Garay López nods his head, and explains: in order to be able to sign the contract for the company for importing wire fencing, with Bianco as co-partner, it has been necessary for him to talk the matter over briefly with his father, since the capital belonging to him through an inheritance from his mother is necessary for him to live – Buenos Aires is a voracious monster that only money pacifies now and again – and only a part of his future inheritance from his father can furnish him with the sums necessary to participate in the company according to the terms agreed upon with Bianco; hence, taking advantage of a leave from the hospital that he has been granted, he has taken the steamer the week before so as to come spend a few days in the city. He has been here since Sunday night, and tomorrow, Thursday, at dusk he will again take the steamer that runs downriver from Paraguay so as to be able to get back to the hospital in time on Sunday, when he is scheduled to be on night duty. But Bianco needn't worry; everything is already all arranged; not only has his father given him the necessary amounts of money, but has even agreed to carry on with the company were something to happen to him, Garay López, and only in that case, and only if Bianco wanted the company to continue. Yesterday afternoon, he and his father went to sign the documents before the proper authorities, so that since the previous afternoon, he and Bianco have been co-partners in the eyes of the law and can begin making their imports, something that makes him, Garay López, proud.

Sunday night! Without allowing it to be apparent, Bianco shivers slightly and his fingers grip the glass of cognac more tightly as he thinks that it was precisely on Sunday night that he left for the country and that perhaps Garay López has been coming to his house every day during his absence, so that the terrible image of Gina puffing on the cigar with her eyes half-closed and an expression of intense pleasure, as Garay López, leaning toward her, speaks to her, smiling at her with a wicked expression, returns to assail Bianco, but loosening the pressure of his fingers a little and taking a sip of cognac, he asks Garay López with impartial interest and an affectionate tone of voice:

"And what about your brother? What was his reaction?"

Garay López's face clouds over. Ah, cher ami, it's impossible to win him over. As happens every time he arrives from Buenos Aires, his brother Juan vanished into the countryside and no doubt he will not appear again until he is quite certain that his brother has gone back to Buenos Aires. Such hatred is inexplicable. He's scarcely more than a boy and he has the entire family terrified; their father has had to muster all his courage in order to make up his mind to sign the contract, because he too is just a little afraid of him. And another of the reasons why his father has agreed to advance him a part of his inheritance is that in his heart of hearts he thinks that, if he should happen to die, Juan would get everything. Not out of avarice, no: out of sheer hatred.

Garay López breaks off, takes a swallow of cognac with a thoughtful expression, and raising his eyes, smiles at him gently:

"But all this is not very interesting. How are things with you? How have your meditations been going?"

Bianco gestures toward the ceiling with his head.

"The rain interrupted them," he says.

Bianco reticently changes the subject: it seems to him that after the scene that he has just come across, talking with Garay López about anything else except the company for importing wire fencing, sharing new confidences as to his plans for refuting the positivists would be to augment his inferiority in relationship to him, to place himself in his power even more in case the scene that he witnessed when he arrived signified what deep down he suspects that it does. And adopting the most jovial tone of voice that he can muster, by making an inordinate effort from amid layers and layers of discouragement and melancholy, he tells him that late that afternoon he has seen a herd of more than two thousand wild horses pass by, doubtless coming from the place in which they spent the winter, and that that has made him think of the urgency of importing wire fencing and of how timely their business venture is.

"Next autumn, I'll be fencing in my lands. When they see the result, they're going to come to us all by themselves to buy wire from us."

"I don't have the least doubt of it," Garay López says.

Bianco looks at him. Garay López's loyalty appears to be sincere. His hair and beard, sleek, coal-black and carefully groomed, surround his pale face and his dark eyes in which there sparkles a penetrating, brilliant gaze, so frank and provocative at times that it seems to border on insolence. Unexpectedly, Garay López breaks off and sets down on the little table the glass in which there still remains a bit of cognac.

"I want to spend this last night with my father and my sisters," he says. "Will we see each other in Buenos Aires?"

"For the moment I don't believe so."

"Maybe next year then. I myself don't think I'll be coming by this way for quite some time. The atmosphere is unhealthy."

Bianco gets to his feet and sees him to the door, leaving behind the warm air of the living room and entering the dark, freezing entry hall. Tied to the hitching post, the horses are patiently standing in the fine rain, not moving except to stamp the mud of the street every so often.

The two men linger in the doorway.

"I'm going to bring the horses in to the stable," Bianco says.

Bianco holds out his hand in a ridiculous gesture, inasmuch as it is invisible in the darkness, but Garay López, with a show of emotion unusual for him, puts his arms around him and presses his chest to his, so swiftly, excessively and firmly, that Bianco, with his arms hanging down his sides, staggers when the other lets go of him, after murmuring to him, almost in his ear:

"It has been a tremendous pleasure, cher ami."

Bianco remains in the doorway for a few minutes, listening to his partner's footsteps die away in the darkness, and then makes up his mind to brave the rain outside so as to bring the horses in.

"This is all I could find," Gina says a little later, serving a potato omelette and taking away the now-empty soup plates so as to pile them up on the sideboard before sitting down at the table again. Cutting two portions of the round omelette and pushing the platter over to Gina for her to serve herself first, Bianco answers her apology by shrugging his shoulders as he pours himself another glass of wine. In the well-lighted calm of the dining room, the couple's movements, repeated day after day at dinner time, are reminiscent of the calculated displacements and the falsely spontaneous gestures of theatrical performances and fill the time that is going by, impalpable and translucent, the way a handful of colored beads fill a transparent glass bottle. Solemnly, her eyes not looking anywhere else, Gina keeps cutting off with the edge of her fork little bits of yellow omelette which she raises absentmindedly to her mouth and slowly chews, with her lips half open, and swallowing only every once in a while after each three or four mouthfuls, until all of a sudden, just as she is picking up a minute piece of yellow pulp, she drops her fork onto her plate and runs out of the dining room. Bianco finds her on the porch, standing motionless in the middle of the stream of light that is coming from the kitchen and that, stretching out toward the patio in the shape of an elongated trapezoid, illuminates a clearly delimited portion of the fine rain that is falling, slow and off-white, on the mosaic tiles. Gina's shoulders are shaking with sobs, and when she hears Bianco approaching, she begins to dry her tears and wipe her nose with the sleeve of her dress. Impenetrable and neutral, Bianco halts alongside her, without touching her, hoping that she will raise her eyes and look at him. In the patio, beyond the porch, the fine rain is falling on their two elongated shadows projected on the paving of mosaic tiles.

"You shouldn't have taken the cigar away from me," Gina says. "I'm still dying of shame."

Bianco wavers between fury and relief. He has followed her out to the porch convinced that, by accepting the fact of her having been caught in a duplicitous intimacy with Garay López, she has decided to own up to the intolerable, and now that he is side by side with her, Gina begins to reproach him for a gesture which, if he remembers correctly, he has made not for the purpose of reprimanding her, but in order to protect her from the smoke that was making her cough. But at the same time he realizes deep down that the expression of pleasure with which Gina was puffing on it just as he opened the door was one of the principal reasons for his stupefaction.

"I did it because you were coughing," Bianco says, feigning surprise and adopting an innocent and protective tone of voice.

Gina's sobs become more high-pitched, more rapid, like an onset of panting, and her hands grip Bianco's shirt and begin tugging on it.

"I have to put up with your business partner all afternoon long, serve him chocolate, cognac, listen to his stupid remarks ..." Gripping his shirt, Gina violently shakes Bianco, making the cadence of her words match each shake, until Bianco forcefully grabs her by the wrists and makes her let go of his shirt. Then, leaning toward her, he asks her, insidiously, in a low voice, almost in her ear:

"Did he say something to you? Did he do something to you?"

"He bores me. I couldn't wait till he left so I could go back to bed again," Gina says, suddenly ceasing to cry.

"You stayed in bed? All day long? All by yourself?" Bianco says.

"Who would you expect me to be with?" Gina says.

"All day by yourself, I mean. Not just all by yourself in bed," Bianco says.

Gina bursts out laughing, putting her arms around him.

"I understand everything backwards," she says. And then, kissing him gently on the cheek: "Don't treat me that way in front of anybody. Don't ever do that again. You frighten me."

"No, no, no," Bianco says in a rapid murmur.

And taking her by the arm, he slowly leads her to the dining room. Making fun, with familiar irony rather than with cruelty, of the eccentricities and the manias of Garay López, they finish dinner. Gina maintains that Garay López, with his pretensions as a dramatist, is rather stingy and is enamored of himself, as is proved by the care with which he grooms and attires himself, with his little beard always well-trimmed and his hair scented and, according to Gina, not a single one of his gestures is spontaneous or free of affectation. But Bianco, surprised by Gina's loquacity, defends him, saying that he's a good doctor, that had it not been for him when he, Bianco, arrived in Buenos Aires, they would have cut his finger off, and that his conversation is most exhilarating. In the middle of his defense of Garay López, Bianco's mood darkens, and he wonders whether Gina, making use of subtle tactics, has not been leading him to a point diametrically opposed to the one in which he ought to have found himself. Noting the obscure fluctuations that his gaze unwittingly betrays, Gina, who has finished clearing the table by piling the dirty dishes on the sideboard for the maids to come and get in the morning, proposes to Bianco that they get to work: and she says that while he was in the country, she has been doing exercises in concentration and that that very afternoon, without going any farther back in time, she has placed a cushion in the middle of the bed, and leaning her shoulders and head on it, has tried to enter into telepathic communication with Bianco. Without awaiting his reply, Gina goes to the drawer of the desk to look for their work tools and deposits them on the polished wooden table.

"I'm too tired to concentrate," Bianco says.

"But this may be the night we'll succeed," Gina says, resting her hand on Bianco's shoulder and shaking him a little, very gently, so as to put an end to his discouragement.

Bianco looks at her and spreads out on the bare table what they call their tools: three cardboard rectangles, all identical, with slightly rounded angles, of a light blue color, like three playing cards, but when Bianco turns them over, instead of the usual figures of decks of cards, three images of a children's game appear, each one representing a different fruit: a walnut, a banana and a bunch of grapes. The images are drawn, in broad, sharp outline, and the designs, more or less stylized, represent each one of the fruits in their simplest, almost geometrical form, against a background of one perfectly uniform color, against which the design stands out clearly. Thus, the walnut, oval in shape and divided into two equal parts by two vertical parallel lines placed very close together, light brown in color on a white background, contains in each one of its two halves several symmetrical curved lines which represent its deep sinuous furrows; the banana, bright yellow, is printed diagonally against a pink background; and the bunch of grapes consists in reality of a multitude of little circles of a blue-violet color, forming in several irregular rows whose number decreases, an inverted triangle, against a bright red background which gives the rough outline of the bunch of grapes a sort of relief. Bianco gets to his feet, taking one last look at the images, and Gina sits down in his place.

Bianco goes into the living room plunged into darkness, and after waiting for a few seconds in order for his eyes to become accustomed to the darkness, he glides without hesitation between the various pieces of furniture and sits down in an armchair. For a few moments still, he performs a series of bodily movements, rotating his shoulder blades, shaking his head to relax the muscles of his neck, pulling on his fingers to make the joints crack, slowly rubbing his eyes, and after covering his face with his hands and immediately afterwards crossing them gently in his lap, he closes his eyes and falls motionless. In the four or five minutes that follow no human sound, apart from Bianco's almost imperceptible breathing, can be heard in the house: only, from time to time, the creaking of the wooden floor, of some piece of furniture, is heard with inconceivable clarity, and not the sound of the fine rain that is falling and enveloping the entire plain in its dense and silent whiteness, but on the other hand there can be heard the sound of the water accumulated in gutters, in trees, in drains, which for some time now has begun to drip or to run in little indecisive and intermittent trickles. Finally Bianco gets to his feet, resolute and bulky, and with no hesitation, as he rumples his brick-colored hair with his whitish hand that gleams in the semidarkness, he crosses the living room and enters the dining room. Gina is seated at the table, with her fingers resting on her breasts and her eyes closed, which open when she hears the door of the living room open. On the table is one of the images, turned over so that only its undifferentiated blue reverse side can be seen. Bianco halts alongside her.

"Bunch of grapes," he says.

Gina shakes her head.

"Walnut," she says, and with two long and delicate fingers turns the card over and shows, on the table, the light brown oval, full of deep symmetrical furrows, standing out against a white background.

When Bianco goes into the bedroom, he notices that, before dinner, Gina has made the bed. The silky bedspread, of a white and green striped fabric, glows in the light of the lamp, and Gina, who appears through the other door, is already in her nightgown, and yawning and stretching, removes the bedspread and slips underneath the coverlet. Calmly, Bianco gets undressed, slowly, meticulously, thinking of the youthful body, full of dark roundnesses, no doubt already slightly warm, which will be against his own body a few minutes later. But when he gets into bed, Gina is already asleep. Bianco contemplates her: Gina's body, that insensate agglomeration of matter, is there before him; he can palpate it with his white hands, already a little rough on the backs, bring it inside his own body by way of his fingertips, his lips, the tip of his tongue, in a congeries of confused and delightful sensations, but what is impalpable there inside it escapes him, that inaccessible breath in which in her new state there are now perhaps cradled incommunicable and unique memories, private sensations that Gina wrenches, with her body, from the thick, avid world. Bianco turns out the light and buries himself between the sheets. When he awakens, the gray morning light is coming in through the skylight. Gina, in her nightdress, is arranging her hair in front of the mirror, and when she notices that his eyes are open, she rivets hers on them in the mirror, and says to him, with conviction and a natural tone of voice: "He came inside me, and without taking it out, made me come twice."

Bianco leaps out of bed, shouting, and Gina wakes up.

"What's the matter?" she says.

Bianco doesn't answer her and buries himself between the sheets again. Murmuring incomprehensible words, Gina gets up and begins to wander around the bedroom in her bare feet. With his head buried in the pillow, his eyes wide open, Bianco hears her pacing hesitantly around the room. The dream that he has just had, and that should have filled him with disgust, with hatred, instead arouses in him an unexpected, intense excitement, to the point that, grabbing his penis with his hand, he squeezes it tightly and turns over, leaning against the headboard of the bed, so as to look at Gina who now, entirely real, has stripped naked in front of the mirror over the washbasin so as to bathe. Gina feels his gaze and sleepily, by way of the mirror, in the same way as in the dream, smiles at him. Bianco is still able to distinguish, inside himself, like two watercourses that are about to meet and intermingle to form just one, the waves of hatred and desire rushing upon him to assault him and destroy him, and tries to go on by focusing on Gina a long, neutral look, without overt intentions or interrogations, but Gina understands, and leaving on top of the washbasin the pitcher that she has just begun to tip toward it, comes over to the bed and flings herself on it face down. Her buttocks swell, smooth, dark, resilient, while the very fine down, on the back of her thighs, slowly stands on end. With her face flattened against the green and white stripes of the bedspread, Gina raises her eyes and sees that Bianco has his eyes riveted on her buttocks. A slow smile, which begins as a mocking one but ends up mingling with dreamy and painful aftertastes, appears in her eyes rather than on her lips. "My cunt," Gina says, strongly emphasizing each one of the syllables in a tone of voice full of surprised irritation, of reproach, finding it unthinkable that that part of her body that to her is remote, indifferent, almost alien, can cause that much fascination in Bianco, but immediately thereafter, and almost in spite of herself, she half-closes her eyes and begins to breathe rapidly and move her tongue, frenetically, inside her mouth, in such a way that the reddish tip of it, that at times appears, fleetingly, outside, inflates and deflates her cheeks, while her lower belly, flattened against the white and green stripes of the bedspread, begins to take on a circular motion that spreads throughout her body, and especially through her round, glossy buttocks. Bianco gets out of bed and strips naked. To hatred, to desire, there is now added terror, the conviction that Gina's desire is independent of, autonomous from his own, like an undulation that comes from farther off than all intentions, all feelings and all resolutions. Seizing her by the shoulders, he turns her over, face up. A vertical streak of down starts from Gina's navel and stretches down across her belly, until it forms with the triangle of her pubis a black arrow that seems to point the way, unmistakably, to the reddish abyss. Bianco enters her. In terror, he lets himself fall against the body that is shaking, a palpitating, fortuitous form, with no other law save that of its own transformations, its chemical appetites, its avid tissues and its humors, material gathered together in ganglia, in nerves, in skin, in smoking blood, and he feels vanquished yet again, with no desire to be alive or to begin once more, a breath imprisoned in the excremental claws of the secondary, until, effacing even his disgust and his vacillations, dragging it for an incalculable time through a black corridor, orgasm ensues, the sudden rain of sperm that frees, fecundates and perpetuates.

At nightfall, the shepherds have gone to sleep, as one of them continues to watch over the flock. After a moment, the one who has been keeping watch comes and shakes the others, speaking in a very loud voice, almost shouting in fact, and very excited: "As you were sleeping an angel came to announce the news to us that a king is being born in Bethlehem, in a stable, and the angel said that, just as we lead the lambs and the goats to pasture, that king will lead us. Wake up, wake up, we must start out for Bethlehem," and the shepherds get up, a little dazed, rubbing their eyes, without quite knowing if they are still awake or still asleep, and they begin walking, feeling their way and stumbling every so often in the darkness, in the direction of Bethlehem. All of a sudden, one of them raises his eyes to the sky, and among all the stars, there is one that appears in the east and, visibly increasing in size, begins to move, the only one among all the others, which remain motionless, anonymous, toward a point in the sky that, the shepherds are certain, is located just above Bethlehem. And a procession that they meet on the way confirms that they are not mistaken, and as they are stepping up their pace a little so as not to lose sight of the procession, they catch up with it and learn that it is made up of three kings come from the Orient with their servants who are also going to Bethlehem, because they have had a similar vision, since, a servant tells the shepherds, an angel descending from heaven has told the kings that just as they rule over their peoples, a child that has just been born in Bethlehem will rule over them, will be the king of kings. And the shepherds join the retinue. The great, luminous star, shifting place often in the sky and following its own path in relationship to the others, which by comparison appear pale, fixed and anonymous, continues to guide them, safely, toward Bethlehem, and along the way, as many others were hoping, struggling, their efforts growing more and more feeble, in the gray net of their days, for an event, an apparition to come at last to get them out of that gray net, peasants, nobles, women, men, those who feel more enervated than their crimes or their hopes, those who would like to go to sleep once and for all and have a nightmare, since to them not being able to sleep either by day or by night is their nightmare, those who in the light of the sun find nothing but hunger, suffering or delirium, those who in the end would like to know whether their presence on these stony white paths that the day turns to ashes obeys chance or a summons, many people, a little sleepy, incredulous, come out of the dark fields to join the group, with their eyes fixed on the star. It is a peasant, a peasant who has just been born in Bethlehem, the peasants murmur among themselves, who just as we work the soil over, will work us over so as to make something greener than darkness and despair sprout from us. Until, still growing a little in size, standing out even more clearly against the background of the others, distant and opaque, the star halts above Bethlehem.

There is a moment of hesitation among the group, since, seeing that the entire village is asleep, nobody, neither kings, nor peasants, nor shepherds, knows where to head. The star seems to point, with its bright blue gleaming rays, to a stable, so that after several secret deliberations, presided over by the three kings, they make their way toward it, and pushing open the wooden door, old and about to fall apart, they go inside. They can see practically nothing in the semidarkness, so they light a torch, and among the moving, fleeting and rather shapeless shadows that the flame projects, they go all through the stable which, apart from some dusty and doubtless unused harnesses, and some straw, spoiled and dried up, scattered all over the floor, is, unmistakably, empty. A murmur runs through the expectant crowd, like a vague wave, two words which some of them do not hear clearly, and which have to be repeated several times, in a low voice and a disappointed or dismayed tone of voice: "It's empty. What's that you say? It's empty." Perhaps we've entered the wrong stable, some of them say, or else we haven't rightly interpreted the sign from the star, which only pointed to Bethlehem and not to any precise stable, this stable, or perhaps the star, in its nonhuman, generic language, by designating "stable," did not mean this stable, but some more general stable, so that kings, peasants and shepherds will begin, thanks to that indication, to search for the real, unique, predestined stable, in which the king of kings, the farm hand of farm hands, the shepherd of shepherds has finally decided to make his appearance. And leaving this generic stable, a mere abstract sign of the real one, they begin to wander through the sleeping town. They divide up into several groups, more and more expectant, anxious, and disoriented, and with growing excitement as well, they begin to search for the stable. The silent village begins to be full of the sound of voices, and little by little of shouts, and in the dancing light of the torches, the groups spread out in the back streets paved with stones, opening the doors of the stables with a certain frenzy, and in certain cases, forcing them open. The people of Bethlehem awaken, coming out of their houses: what is that noise, that uproar, the village dwellers ask each other, until they come upon the kings, who, followed by a small crowd, without paying any attention to them, are breaking down the door of a stable in which nothing is to be found except for two or three listless animals half asleep. We're kings from the Orient, the kings explain to the stupefied villagers, and we have come to Bethlehem following that star, because with its incandescent points it is signifying to us that, in one of the stables, a king has just been born of whom we, the kings, are the acknowledged subjects, a shepherd who, day and night, will shepherd the shepherds. The people of Bethlehem burst out laughing. Whoever told you such a wild story? There hasn't been anybody born in the village, you may ask anyone you like, there has been no birth registered for several weeks now, moreover: not one birth or death. And they, the inhabitants of Bethlehem, have proof, in case the strangers won't take their word for it: just yesterday, by order of Cyrenius, the governor of Syria, who in turn had orders from Augustus Caesar, had had a tax list, a census made, and all the villagers had been registered, counted, and counted again, and the figures were precisely those predicted, nobody had been born or had departed from this world since the order for the census had arrived, nobody had gotten out of registering, everyone was included on the list. The inhabitants of Bethlehem, without losing their calm because of the intrusion of the strangers, raise their heads and gaze at the sky. The star is a big one, it is true, a little bigger than usual as a matter of fact, but it doesn't look disproportionately large. In Babylonia and in Chaldea, they already had exact knowledge of the sky, and they didn't see all that many omens either in the brilliance, or the path, or the size of the stars. And moreover, those points that the strangers are trying to interpret as a sign, do not give them, the inhabitants of Bethlehem, who have the good luck of enjoying a clear sky (a piece of luck that perhaps they lack in the Orient), though those points of the star are, as a matter of fact, very luminous tonight, the impression that they are designating anything, any stable in particular, not even

Bethlehem to tell the truth, since at the altitude at which the
star is located in relation to the village, it would be too fool-
hardy to maintain the contrary. No, no, what they have taken as
an omen is an isolated fact, the vision of angels that kings and
shepherds have had, a dream, a pleasant one, to be sure, but no
more tangible than a phantasmagoria, and the increase in size,
the luminosity and the path of the star, just above the road and
in the fields where they were, a mere coincidence. Look, look:
since dawn is approaching, the star has begun to move backwards. It is not very noticeable yet, but in a little while it will be
more perceptible, and when dawn finally comes, undeniable.
The kings, the shepherds and the peasants, gathered in little
groups and perplexed after contemplating the sky for a moment,
cannot convince themselves that the star is moving backwards.
The villagers of Bethlehem smile among themselves: they are
peasants, of course, shepherds, while the kings come from the
Orient, where people are too credulous, a bit backward; they
have a disoriented look in their eyes, and though ignorant, they
seem to be men of good will; let us open all the stables in
Bethlehem so that they'll be convinced.

And that is what they do. With somewhat ostentatious toler-
ance and a rather theatrical acquiescence, the inhabitants of
Bethlehem open to the strangers not only the doors to all their
stables, but also of all their inns and hostelries, and even of their
own houses, showing them all the rooms, and uncovering and at
times raising in their arms so that they can get a good look at
them, all the babies born in the last few months, to demonstrate
that there is not a single newborn among them, not a one who
has on its head the mark of any sort of predestination, that none
of them is anything more than the plump offspring of trades-
men, craftsmen or publicans, until, convinced at last, the
strangers go out into the streets again, where the night is beginning to grow pale. They may search wherever they like, the

people of Bethlehem tell them before going back to bed, we're leaving you the keys, go to the farmhouses in the vicinity, to the neighboring towns, say that we've sent you and they will open all their doors to you. When the strangers are by themselves again, the air is ash-gray and frigid; on raising their heads they notice that the star has disappeared, taking its place once again among the others, pale, distant, ice-cold, and that it is impossible to recognize it among the multitude of incomprehensible and vaguely luminous points which the morning brightness is beginning to blot out. Without a word, they disperse, the peasants to work the soil before the sun begins to scorch it, to dry it out again, the shepherds to look for the herds that, with a bit of luck, are perhaps waiting for them, patient and trusting, without scattering, the kings, with their useless presents, to begin the journey homeward. In the ash-gray air, their ashen faces are barely visible, against a background of ash-colored stones, which the rising sun, indifferent and cyclical, will soon turn blinding white as it becomes incandescent, it too the fleeting fruit of other coincidences no less neutral and transitory.

Bianco is somewhat perplexed. It is not yet a week since he got off the boat and already he is eating in the hotel restaurant with Doctor Garay López, nearly fifteen years younger than he, the physician who has lanced the abscess on his finger, standing up to the head doctor of the hospital who wanted to amputate. Garay López, who, when he has gone to see him for the second time two days later to have the wound cleaned and the bandages changed, has talked to him of Paracelsus and Pythagoras, has recited to him in their original languages verses from Coleridge and from Baudelaire, the latter a poet scarcely known except by a few unwavering supporters among whom he, Bianco, does not count himself, has proposed to him that they have dinner together, and when they have finished eating, has related to him in detail, mixing together, as appears to be his habit, French,

English and Italian, his theatrical allegory, as he calls it, in seven tableaux, entitled *The Magi*, with great conviction and even a somewhat histrionic exuberance in his gestures, exaggerating on purpose so as to deride himself, although now that he has ended his recital, sitting back motionless in his chair, he rivets, with just a touch of anxiety, his big black eyes on Bianco's, trying to divine in them the effect that his project of literary creation has produced on him.

In all truth, Bianco's judgment and even his interest as far as literature is concerned are rather limited, not to say nonexistent, and he calls literature anything printed in newspapers, magazines and books having to do with the one subject that strikes him as important, the relationships between mind and matter, deeming good all those works that support the preeminence of mind over matter and bad all those that maintain the contrary, but even though Garay López's theatrical allegory appears to belong more to the second category than to the first, Bianco, out of politeness, since Garay López has shown such interest in the infection in his finger and treated it with such solicitude, and because he is the only person he has to talk to in this immense, unknown continent, he abstains from pronouncing a definite judgment and offers an ambiguous opinion amid lengthy pauses and calculated hesitations. There is, he says, possibly an excess of materialism in his conception.

Garay López relaxes, a condescending smile on his face:

"You're wrong, cher ami. Art is neither materialistic nor spiritualistic: it simply *is*."

Bianco nods, although he has not understood Garay López's argument very clearly and although at heart he completely disagrees with what it seems to him that he has understood, but he feels satisfied that Garay López has not been offended by his objection since, a little stunned by the devastating summer of Buenos Aires, the doctor's company and his slightly meandering conversation not only afford him a distraction, but also provide him with information regarding his imminent settlement on the pampas, information that is of great usefulness to him. Above all since, on his second visit to the hospital, two days before, both have realized, with that joyful astonishment that certain workings of chance provide, that Bianco's lands, south of the Salado River, in the northern region of the pampas, border on those of the Garay López family. After that euphoric discovery, and after all the offers of help needed to get Bianco settled, Garay López's gaze, as he is finishing bandaging Bianco's ring finger for the second time, clouds over a little. And now that they have finished dining in the hotel restaurant, Bianco, intrigued by this change of mood, is awaiting the chance to bring up the subject again in order to try to sound out Garay López. Unexpectedly, it is the latter who, after lighting a cigar and puffing on it for a moment with a thoughtful air, returns to the subject.

"You're going to ask me what I'm doing in Buenos Aires, when my entire family and my lands are a hundred leagues from here," he says, showing himself, by the expression on his face, ready to share confidences.

"I wouldn't allow myself such an indiscretion," Bianco lies, less out of hypocrisy than because it seems to him unnecessary to give signs of too much interest since, in any event, he is almost certain that Garay López's confession will soon be forthcoming.

"I was suffocating to death in that city. When I turned eighteen, I managed to get them to send me to study in Europe. Between Paris, London and Rome, I spent seven years over there. And since, when I came back last year, after spending a month with my family, I felt more suffocated than before I left, I decided to settle in Buenos Aires."

Bianco listens in silence, the backs of his white hands covered with sparse, reddish hairs resting listlessly on the tablecloth, amid breadcrumbs and pale wine stains on the yellow fabric. With an attentive expression that none the less is almost distant, into which he tries to inject, in the most natural way possible, the maximum understanding and nonjudgmental belief, he nevertheless is wondering what these generalities that have assumed the air of intimate confidences are abstaining from expressing, until he realizes that Garay López, in fact constrained by what appears to be Bianco's excessively naïve acceptance, is awaiting a more active interest on his part in order to go on.

"I believe I've experienced similar problems," Bianco says.

Garay López leans toward him, shaking his head slightly to disperse the smoke from his cigar.

"Family problems?" he murmurs, lowering his voice, casting a swift glance toward the other tables, more concerned about safeguarding Bianco's discretion than about preserving his own.

Bianco makes a vague gesture, that might suggest a great many things at once, a negative or its contrary, a bit uncivil in its ambiguity, which instead of augmenting Garay López's discretion kindles, in the most unforeseen way, for the first time, that spark of insolence, inspired in him by Bianco's hazy past, and which with time will become more and more bold, aimed perhaps at exasperating him and forcing him to abandon his circumspection. But something even more unforeseen happens: Bianco's reserve, instead of reducing Garay López to silence, causes him to become more frank, and even more talkative, as though that reserve did away with the dignity of his own life and even its most personal details could be made public, with no limits. He is still almost an adolescent, beginning to grow older without having completely matured within himself, Bianco thinks, hearing him speak volubly, almost cynically, of his own family.

According to Garay López, what stifles him is not only his native city, that flat and widely scattered settlement on the banks of the great river, that city that is like a desert lost among the islands teeming with snakes and crocodiles, and where not only old maids or men far along in years, with no other occupation save to wait for death, spy on you from behind the windows, but also the pretty heiresses who hardly know how to spell out their ABCs and the twenty-year-old men who need only to get themselves a diploma thanks to their relations in Córdoba or in Buenos Aires to be sure that twenty years later they will occupy the governor's chair; not only the city, with its miserable and anonymous outskirts where the terrible summer dries up the garbage and the carrion, with the patios of the rich who are all related to each other and who between them are the owners of almost all of the pampas on which all they have to do is let their herds multiply in order to multiply their fortunes, not only the city, Garay López continues, although the evenings with nobody, absolutely nobody to talk to, with whom to compare a thought, a state of mind that differs slightly from what those who possess everything have decided that everyone ought to think or feel, those nameless nights, invariably melancholy and empty, would be enough to wish upon that nonexistent settlement that has the impudence to call itself a city the same fate as that of Nineveh and Sodom.

"From that point of view all cities are alike," Bianco interrupts him. "Paris, London, Rome. All of them."

"Perhaps," Garay López says, without seeming to have listened to him. And then, as though to himself: "Perhaps."

But not only the city: it's the family especially, the father, the two sisters, the younger brother. His mother, he says, died while she was giving birth to his brother. Garay López lowers his voice as he readies himself to say something, not out of discretion but as though suffocated by a groan of hatred that makes him lean forward a little, half-close his eyes, and stare at Bianco from head to foot, as though because of what he is about to say, he were preparing himself to receive the blow which will inevitably be dealt him in answer to the phrase he is about to utter: "One does not give birth with impunity to an arsonist."

On hearing it, Bianco moves his head slightly and looks at the empty dark glass bottle of wine that is standing on the table. Garay López guesses what he is thinking and bursts out laughing:

"No, cher ami. Don't blame my indignation on an addiction to alcohol."

"No. I just wanted to order another one," Bianco says.

"A cognac," Garay López says.

They order a cognac. The nearly unbearable heat of the street is more unbearable still in the restaurant, and the cognac makes Garay López's forehead break out in little yellowish drops that begin to slide down his cheeks and disappear, leaving behind sinuous tracks on his cheeks, in his black beard. A customer shouts to one of the waiters to open the doors to let a little air in, and since it is still early, the conversation, the sound of voices, take on a certain relief against a loud background of horses' hoofs and of wheels of vehicles that hit against, or noisily clatter over the paving stones. I am measuring my words: an arsonist, Garay López says. I am almost convinced of it.

And he tells him the story. On the pampas, property deeds are vague, and the cattle ranchers make use of the land as though the entire province belonged to them. This is the way things have been for a century now, ever since they began to exploit the wild cattle and domesticate them. And when they manage to make the Indians retreat a few leagues, the lands taken over are shared between three or four families. Governors, magistrates, bishops, military officers come from these same families. Their members intermarry and multiply in the same way as their herds of cattle. His own family is practically the most powerful one in those parts. The governor is an uncle of his, his mother's brother. Multiplying themselves and their cattle, enlarging their land holdings: that is all that interests them. His own father could have been governor, but after the death of Garay López's mother, he lives in retirement, terrified by the idea of death and by his own son, who has tyrannized him ever since he was thirteen or fourteen years old. His brother Juan is the one who rules over the house, who lays down the law. Since he grew up without a mother, his father, out of compassion in the beginning and out of fear a little later on, has completely given in to him. And now he is the slave of his own son, an irascible and capricious tyrant twenty years old.

When his mother died giving birth to Juan, Garay López was seven years old. He too, he says, has grown up without a mother, and yet he never has given in to fits of rage, to violence as has Juan, who from the time he first began to walk had everyone terrified: maidservants, friends, relatives. He was ill-tempered, cold, reserved. As early as the age of ten he would disappear into the countryside for days on end, engaging in cruel pastimes, alone in the middle of the pampas, with a knife longer than his arm crossed at his waist, tucked diagonally across his kidneys, and a carbine in his hand, going all over the countryside on horseback and sleeping in the open. When he was fifteen, as one of his sisters had told Garay López in a letter, he ordered the ranch hands around with a whiplash and even this early in his life, men thirty, forty years old, able to slit with one stroke the throat of anyone who stared at them for a moment too long, were afraid of him and at the same time adored him like a god. They would have unhesitatingly allowed themselves to be killed for him. The day before, he, Garay López, received a visit from one of them, a cutter of the throats of Indians who, twirling his sombrero nervously with the tips of his fingers, almost in tears, asked him to intercede for him with his brother, because Juan, for no discernible reason, had ordered him thrown off the ranch, telling him that he didn't want to see him anywhere in the vicinity again. With Garay López, relations, during their childhood and on his return from Europe, the year before, had been difficult, not to say nonexistent. He, in his childhood, had pitied Juan, that baby he had seen still covered with blood from the womb of his dying mother. But Juan accepted neither affection nor his pity. It was impossible to penetrate his thoughts, and if he had ever had a sorrow in his life, it must have been, even to himself, obscure, incomprehensible, ignored, forgotten inside him as being a sorrow and showing itself on the outside in the form of silent rancor, inordinate pride and violence.

Because of the cognac and perhaps the meal, of the hot and muggy atmosphere that seems to accumulate in his nose and throat, in the hotel restaurant in which, despite the open doors, there is not a breath of air, Bianco deduces that drops of sweat like those that are forming on Garay López's forehead must be running down his own back, since his shirt is clinging to his skin, in which a sort of damp tickling feeling is moving from place to place. And he thinks: "If what he tells about the customs of the region are true, a person wonders whether the brother doesn't have every reason in the world to be impossible to deal with." But after hesitating a bit, since Garay López has surmised that a thought has just crossed his mind, he comments:

"Your part of the country doesn't seem very hospitable."

"The country is innocent, cher ami," Garay López says. "The problem lies with those who live in it."

And he stares at him for a moment.

Bianco slowly shakes his head, with a deliberately ambiguous expression, which Garay López notes and understands, because, shaking his head in turn with a sarcastic little laugh, assumes for the second time during dinner that insolent expression that, even though it makes Bianco slightly irritated, is in reality a sort of acquiescence.

They speak in French, in English, in Italian. Every so often, in just one language, for several sentences, then larding into one of them set phrases or exclamations from the other two, and at moments when the dialogue becomes a little more animated, in the three languages at once. Every so often, Bianco will venture to utter some phrase or other in Spanish, in order to demonstrate that, in spite of the fact that barely a week after having disembarked on these flat and scorching-hot shores, he is not about to allow himself to stray into the invisible traps that the language sets for him and that he has already begun to practice speaking it, with a hesitant pronunciation, and with the peculiar accent he has in all the other languages, including his mother tongue.

"And those who live in it..." Garay López says and breaks off for a moment, deep in thought.

He takes a sip of cognac and goes on: everything could have gone on that way, he says, until the end of time. But the national government had the idea, nobody knows why, and you, cher ami, may perhaps know the reason better than I do, of bringing farmers from Europe and giving them state lands and having them grow wheat, and things like that, do you follow me?, thinking that if the wife of the President of the Republic should find it necessary some day to travel to the provinces in the interior, she and the group accompanying her could stay at one or another of those little land holdings and sleep there overnight before arriving at their destination. The fact is that, along with their families, a few Italians, some Swiss, two or three Asturians have settled in the region and begun to grow wheat, Garay López says. To grow wheat, he adds, on a strip of land that the national government had granted them, but that, through one of those unfortunate coincidences, fell just within the boundaries of some pastureland that his own family, the Garay

Lópezes, considered their own, although, to tell the truth, it was not shown on any official land register. The grass of the region isn't the best on the pampas; there is too much clay in the soil, which keeps rainwater from being absorbed; but the grass of the family pasturelands is none the less of good quality, and that on this fringe of land, the rightful ownership of which is still up in the air, almost as good as that in the south of the province of Buenos Aires, to which the national government is not sending a single immigrant, for the simple reason that those lands belong to none other than the members of the government. According to Garay López, Juan had gone to speak with his uncle, the governor, whose answer was, according to Garay López: my dear nephew, times change, I can't back down on the issue because, in fact, in order to accept those immigrants, I asked the government to grant me in exchange some good pasturelands south of the Carcarañá River, and they were granted to me, an agreement that you ought to feel pleased about since those lands now belong to the family, but according to Garay López, Juan didn't want to have anything to do with the deal, and he warded off with a clack of his whip the penpusher from the Department of the Interior who wanted to see him to the door. In the beginning, the immigrants did not let themselves be intimidated either by the pressure put on them or by the threats against them, and settled down to grow wheat, period. Even though it's not as good as the land in the south of the province of Buenos Aires, that strip of land of uncertain ownership is good enough to produce two wheat harvests a year, Garay López says. It requires hard work, even sacrifices, but it returns them with interest – or so I've heard tell, Garay López says with his usual little laugh, since as you can see for yourself, these hands (and he holds them out in front of him, palms up, above the glasses of cognac and the dishes in which the remains of the meal are getting cold) haven't worked the land much in their twenty-seven years of existence. But when the first crop of wheat was ripe, all ready to be harvested, a fire broke out which completely destroyed it. It's true that it was a very dry year and that accidents like that often happen, but as if by chance, the next three harvests met a similar fate: the following one, when the wheat had already been cut and brought in, ready to be sent to the city; and the other two, two or three days before the harvest. After the fourth accident, the peasants, finally understanding the warning, abandoned the fields and went back, some to the city, others to Buenos Aires, and still others to Switzerland or Spain. Since then, the strip of land has been abandoned, and my family's cattle once again peacefully chew on that juicy grass.

"A series of unfortunate coincidences," Bianco says.

"I thank you for your tactfulness," Garay López says.

But, to tell the truth, the story has not impressed him. Viewing it from a distance, he is wondering why the brother chose that solution, the last one that he, Bianco, would have chosen, thinking at the same time that he has too much common sense to go to such extremes, and with the swiftness of a strategist who two minutes later must send his troops out onto the battlefield, runs through a whole series of intermediate solutions that he would have adopted which would have genuinely satisfied not only him but the peasants as well. And all of this without any sort of psychological projection regarding the peasants, or any humanitarian concern, but simply considering the immigrants as yet another factor in a practical problem requiring a solution, in the same way as when the consul in Agrigento offered him a job in exchange for land, and he began to travel all over Italy to enlist peasants in the adventure, at no time did his activity seem to him anything else but the inevitable phase of a process that would permit him, Bianco, to settle in a region of the planet far enough away to enable him to escape the scandal and remote enough to be able to offer him a good situation to ensure his having the leisure he required for his refutation of the positivists. And thinking also: this family is the richest one in the province because it has devoted itself to cattle raising. Therefore, he must devote himself to raising cattle.

Garay López, feeling contented because of the confidences he has shared, or perhaps the cognac, or the evening in general, the beginning of which he has spent recalling memories of Paris, London, Rome, leans back a little in his chair, and taking his last puffs on his cigar, amid a cloud of grayish smoke, stubs it out on the plate, amid the remains of food, cold now, and after making sure that there is not a single shred of tobacco still alight, raises his smiling if slightly melancholy gaze toward Bianco.

"I'm boring you with these family stories," he says, and putting his hand in his pocket takes out his watch.

"On the contrary, they're most instructive," Bianco says, seeing Garay López opening the watch case, look at the time, raise the watch to his ear, shake it several times, trying to hear it tick, winding it and raising it to his ear once more and shaking it again several times until, with a resigned expression, he is about to put it back into his pocket.

"It's broken," he says.

Bianco extends his open hand toward it, and with an obedient but surprised gesture, Garay López deposits it on his palm. The silver watch, closed, flat, is resting on the open palm of Bianco's right hand, grazing the edge of the bandage on his right finger that Garay López himself has changed for him the previous day. Bianco leans his palm slightly in Garay López's direction to afford him a good look at the watch and his palm, which has remained open the whole time, until after a few seconds' transition, during which he remains motionless and rigid, with his eyes half closed, he extends the index and the middle finger of his left hand and slowly rotates them a few centimeters above the watch, without touching it, describing in the air tighter and tighter circular motions, as though, to tell the truth, rather than circles, his two closely joined outstretched fingers were describing a spiral in the air. Finally he stops, opens his eyes, and hands Garay López his watch back with a ceremonious gesture. Garay López opens the case, looks at the watch face, checks the time by means of the clock that is hanging on a wall of the restaurant, raises the watch to his ear with a smile, nodding his head, and then, closing the watch case, puts it back in his pocket again.

"Great stuff, cher ami."

Bianco shrugs. When they leave the restaurant, it is already past midnight, but the air is still hot and close, and after walking for a few meters, they take off their suit coats, roll up their shirt sleeves, and each of them holding his suit coat by the neck with one finger, letting it dangle down his back over one shoulder, or carrying it folded across a forearm, they head for the river.

"In my province," Garay López says, "a man's footsteps lead him instinctively to the river."

In the city plunged into semidark shadows, every so often they meet a number of bodies, a little darker still, moving about in the deep shadow. Every so often also, on the sidewalks, is a family sitting in chairs or on the doorsills, fighting against going off to bed, stubbornly insisting on wanting to breathe the cool air, purely imaginary, of the hours before the sun comes up. When the two of them reach the riverbank, they see two or three lanterns slowly moving about, mirrored by the water, and Bianco smells for the first time in his life, he who at forty thought he had smelled every odor, the very special one of the river, full of the smell of unknown fish, of watersoaked clay, of decayed plants, of underwater carrion, of earth leveled or eaten away.

"Fishermen," Garay López says, alluding to the duplicated

lights moving horizontally in the semidarkness on the nearly invisible river. And then he tells him that, when he comes to the hospital to have the bandage on his ring finger changed, he will give him letters of introduction to his family.

But on the following day, when Bianco has just awakened, around eleven in the morning, his brick-red hair soaking wet and stuck to his temples, the sheets wet with sweat, the inordinately bright yellow morning light entering through the slats in the shutters, knocks at the door bring him out of his puzzling half-sleep, and when he asks who it is, Garay López's voice answers him in jovial French:

"I know all about your troubles. But don't worry. I'll be as silent as the tomb."

And when he enters the room, a bit excited, giving Bianco scarcely time enough to get dressed, he spreads out on the table three or four French magazines dating from the year before, full of long articles on Bianco's run-in with the positivists, articles that he, Bianco, has already read and reread fifty times, with rage, with self-contempt, with resentment, with murderous intentions and with desperation as well. One magazine has even featured him on the cover, a huge colored caricature in which Bianco, shown as a chubby figure with pencil-thin arms and legs, a prominent breast and belly and a huge head on which his red hair is represented by a turbulent flareup of bright flames, is gazing in bewilderment at a clown who, atop Big Ben, is performing above the face of the clock the same spiral motion that he has employed the night before over Garay López's watch. For a few seconds, forgetting Garay López, the present, the world, his own being, Bianco turns into a blind boiling over of humiliation and rage, until, with great effort, he begins to murmur to himself, calm, calm, I have come to bury myself here for the express purpose of refuting all that, I have a trunkful of books and the strength of my thought is still intact, and when he raises his eyes, or opens them, or without having either lowered them or closed them, simply begins to see the outside world again, as the boiling over of rage and shame surges back once more, he finds before him Garay López's grave face, into whose cheeks, so deliberately pale, two reddish patches have mounted, and whose mouth, amid his thick black beard, smooth and well-trimmed, has dropped open in surprise and is trembling slightly.

"Excuse me," Garay López says. "I didn't think you'd react that way."

"That way? What do you mean by that?" Bianco answers, laughing, and putting the magazines back into a neat pile, with calculated calm, gratified to see that his hands aren't trembling. "I'm merely surprised to note that we can count on having news from Europe in these remote backlands. Pleasantly surprised."

If he had really been a Prussian spy, would he have come to bury himself in the midst of the pampas? The positivist cabal in Paris had shown, by launching these calumnies, their inability to refute with genuinely scientific arguments the reality of his powers, powers that he, far from using them for his personal aims, had had the naïveté and the good faith to place at the disposal of those people. He himself, for years, had not believed in his power – in our century, doctor, we are born positivists, and only later, and if we're lucky, do a few of us stumble sometimes on more solid and more enlightening truths. Except that, out of obtuse obstinacy, if a person comes across those truths, he may confine himself to the mere appearance of matter. Matter is the corollary of mind; what we believe we perceive we merely represent to ourselves; we represent to ourselves the rough surface, and we represent to ourselves the tips of our fingers with which we believe that we are touching something rough.

As he goes on talking, Bianco observes, with rapid, furtive glances, Garay López's reaction, which without the slightest doubt is satisfactory since for a time now, nodding his head in approval, Garay López prepares to say something that probably confirms and even reinforces Bianco's words, but he contains himself in order not to interrupt him, so that Bianco, in order to verify his observation, ends his sentence and falls silent, giving him a chance to reply.

"That is what I've noticed at medical school," Garay López says. "That's the favorite joke of my colleagues: I'm never going to be able to come across the soul when I'm doing dissections."

But he, Garay López, who has spent eight years poking about in human organs, knows that the soul is not to be sought among those viscera but in the hand that manipulates the scalpel.

"That soul without which there is no scalpel," Bianco says, and then immediately: "Since you were kind enough to invite me to dinner last night, will you permit me to invite you to lunch in whatever is your favorite place?"

And they go out into the street, at noon on a summer day. Bianco notes again, in the flat, straight streets, the presence of the countryside, not only in the vacant lots, in the patios and in the gardens, but in the very atmosphere, in the layout of the houses, in the streets of beaten earth, in the spaces between the paving stones, in which, despite the traffic of vehicles and horses, the grass springs up, flexible and persistent, and the tufts ramify. But also in something indefinable, in the façades of the houses of unwhitewashed brick, in the unmistakable sensation that all of this is recent, precarious, and that seen from the pampas, the settlement laid out in this pattern of regular squares, must look like a flat, laughably paltry clutter and even a mirage. When they have gone a few blocks, a man crosses the street from the opposite sidewalk and plants himself in front of them, smiles at them, speaking Italian, and keeps them from going any farther. It takes Bianco several seconds to recall where he has seen that face before, until he recognizes the man as a Calabrian who came over on the boat with him, and with whom he had a conversation one night when strolling on the lower deck.

"How are they treating you, ilustrissimo?" the Calabrian asks.

"All right for the moment," Bianco replies. "And how about you?"

The Calabrian makes a vague gesture, shrugging and smiling faintly, a gesture that might mean that the situation is uncertain, but that he is prepared to accept whatever comes his way.

"The family?" Bianco says.

"Down at the port," the Calabrian says.

"Still?" Bianco says.

The Calabrian makes a gesture consisting of rapidly rubbing together the tips of his index finger and his thumb, to signify that he has no money.

"Luckily, the weather's warm. A person can sleep out of doors," the Calabrian says.

Bianco takes out some banknotes, and puts them in the upper part of the man's jacket, though the Calabrian puts up an embarrassed resistance, twisting and turning a little so as to try to keep the banknotes from being tucked into his pocket.

"A thousand thanks, ilustrissimo," he finally says, standing still so as to let Bianco slip the bills in.

Taking off his sombrero and putting it back on, the man says goodbye, accompanying his gesture with a slight bow. "The one way to get really rich, without problems, in this country or in any other, is to have the poor on one's side," Bianco thinks, beneath the discreet but admiring gaze of Garay López, who, to tell the truth, ever since he has known him, appears to be ready to grant him an unlimited amount of affection, for rather obscure reasons, perhaps appertaining to Garay López's character and that, after all, Bianco not only does not find completely unjustified, but on the contrary takes a certain pleasure in, a sort of confidence in himself or in his lucky star, in the days and the years to come, and also in this young man with a coal-black head of hair and a beard that are sleek and well-trimmed, dressed in an elegant suit of Havana-colored linen, at least a head taller than he, who is now strolling at his side along the uneven sidewalks beneath a blue sky so cloudless that it is turbulent, which the sun, not far from the zenith, is piercing with its harsh, incandescent, fluctuating beams.

"You now understand why I raised certain objections to your ... how do you call it? Your piece on the Magi?"

"A theatrical allegory," Garay López says.

"Theatrical allegory. That's it," Bianco says. "I seemed to perceive in it, at least as you describe it, aftertastes of the abominable materialism of this century. I too fight the gods, but in the name of the mind. They too bear the mark of matter."

"You can't have any idea how close I feel you to be to my own thought," Garay López says.

"As close, I hope," Bianco says jovially, rubbing his hands together, "as we are to the restaurant."

He spends all summer in Buenos Aires, in the first place because the official and definitive registration of his lands in the north takes more time than he had foreseen, and also because Garay López advises him against moving there in summer, because of the heat – still worse than in Buenos Aires, Garay López says, worse than anything you can imagine, in days in January one feels even more forsaken, more lost, more unreal; if even in the temperate season life appears to be unreasonable and empty, in the summer months the state of men and things weakens and everything, slightly feverish and exhausted, tends toward mass destruction. Faced with these statements, Bianco knits his reddish eyebrows slightly and a skeptical smile appears on his lips, accentuating their bitter convulsive contraction: he, Bianco, as he habitually answers Garay López, is as indifferent to winter as to summer, to clear days as to cloudy ones, droughts mean no more to him than downpours, he is always exactly the same, indifferent to the changes in the outside world, and has only one objective: to settle as soon as possible on his lands, south of the Salado River, let loose some cattle on this land, and devote the majority of his time to thought, to abstraction, to the elaboration, clear and well-conceived, of a system that will finally demolish the errant nonsense of the positivists and to recovering the full use of his powers which, he must admit, the events in Paris have somewhat weakened.

So at the end of March he goes upriver in a little steamboat that makes its way along slowly, shuddering, loaded with bundles and with passengers – Italians, Basques whose job is to dig in the earth, Irish, a consumptive Frenchman – and two days later he disembarks in the city.

"It doesn't give me the impression of being the Sodom that you described," he will write, in French, the following week to Garay López, "but I admit that the autumn is still hot. I now understand why there are no mosquitoes either in London, or in Berlin, or in Paris: the quantity buzzing in the air around me as I write exhausts the productive capacity of Mother Nature. All the individuals of the species seem to be holding their annual congress tonight. Or perhaps this city is the Babylon of mosquitoes. I have found a room in the inn that you told me about and the Spaniard's wife cooks fairly well. There is a magnificent patio; the oranges will be ripe in about a month. I still haven't gone to have a look at my property, nor have I permitted myself to call on your family, where I am certain that, thanks to your kind letter of introduction, I will be well-received. I am taking my time. I stroll about the city a great deal, and I do not see in it, I repeat, the satanic attributes that a certain overly sensitive young doctor whom I met in Buenos Aires, maintains that he finds when he wanders about the streets. I realize that not many diversions await me, but for the time being my one concern is to acquire an intimate acquaintance with the place that will doubtless be my center of operations in the years to come. As for Buenos Aires, apart from your intelligent and most useful company, I miss only certain young ladies who, out of concern as a hygienist, you had the good sense to see to it that I met."

To tell the truth, if he has not yet gone to visit the Garay Lópezes, it is because he wants the official documents of the province to show exactly the location, the boundaries, and the precise measurements of his property before going to acquaint himself with it; he wants to arrive at it as the definite owner, to speak with Juan as an equal, to give him to understand that, if they are neighbors and if he, Bianco, decides some day to rent out his lands to peasants so that they can grow wheat, the bad luck of the repeated fires that have destroyed harvests will not discourage him the way they did the small landholders of the year before, and also because it seems prudent to him to have a look at the Garay Lópezes from afar, to know something more about them before beginning to see a good deal of them, convinced, ever since his obscure years, that, in every relationship, the one who knows the most about the other is in a position of strength, has superior knowledge, and can profit from what he knows. Hence one rainy night after dinner, he invites the Spaniard over to his table when all the other customers have left, and the two of them begin chatting together. The Spaniard has lived in the city for years; for years he had been a tenant farmer on a little piece of land east of Córdoba, but a couple of seasons of torrential rains and another of drought ruined his harvests, so he decided to leave the countryside. A Basque proposed to him that they leave their families in Córdoba and go dig ditches in the south for a season. Those who are part Spanish don't want to dig in the ground; they think that it is dishonorable labor. And the only way that they have – with the word "they" and a vague movement of his head the Spaniard designates the entire region – to set the boundary lines for property, for herds of cattle and for Indians, is to dig ditches. It is killing work. In a single season, he ruined his hands and his lower back, but since nobody in the region wants to dig, it is also work that is well-paid. Work for brute beasts, the Spaniard says, for Irishmen or for Basques. Look at the condition it left my hands in, and I worked at it for just one season, more than ten years ago. Bianco looks at his hands, that do not look too badly ruined, but in which the Spaniard seems to store his memories, as others do in a reliquary. With the money they earned digging ditches that season, the Basque bought a pasture and a whole flock of sheep, and he for his part came to the city to set up the inn. Bianco pours him another brandy, and the Spaniard accepts only after making certain, with furtive glances that rapidly survey the entire room, that his wife is nowhere in the vicinity. The Garay Lópezes?, he says, answering Bianco's question with another question. And then, lowering his voice: they're the owners of everything. The older son is a doctor, but he lives in Buenos Aires. Nobody got along with his brother. The father is very ill; his nerves, it seems. It is Juan, the younger brother, who manages the ranch. When he is in the city, he sometimes comes to eat at the inn. In the morning he orders them to prepare a special dish for him and he turns up that night with four or five bums and two or three women of ill repute, girls from the outskirts of town, and they stay on, eating, drinking and playing cards till dawn. The Spaniard's wife can't stand him; she prepares the dish he's ordered in the afternoon, leaves it in the oven for the servant to warm up, and goes off with the kids to one of the neighbors. He, the Spaniard, has seen him drunk more than once: he goes rigid, his eyes glaze over, and his face sets in an evil expression. He is twenty years old, and he is already almost completely bald. It is hard to get a word out of him; he settles everything with blows of his whip. He goes in and out of the Department of the Interior as though it were his own house. He gets along better with his uncle the governor, people say, than with his own father, who is afraid of him. Twenty years old, can you imagine?, the Spaniard says. He lowers his voice again and casts his furtive glances all around the room to make certain that his wife is nowhere in the vicinity. He whores around a lot, he says. He could have the prettiest young girls in the province, pair off with them, all of them clean and nice-looking, fourteen or fifteen years old, who would be happy if he got them pregnant, but he prefers harlots, much older than he is; they say, the Spaniard says, that he has two or three sent to him at the ranch for him alone. When virgins arrive at the brothel, he gets first crack at them; and always goes back to the oldest ones, the ugliest ones, the most worn-out ones. You should see him ride through the streets on horseback; his skin tanned almost black, his bald head peeling from exposure to the sun, which makes him a bit embarrassed and he seldom takes off his sombrero, lost in thoughts that make his eyes gleam with rancor. And out on the pampas, always on horseback there too, with the cowhands from the ranch, a bunch of animals, the Spaniard says, illiterate brutes who don't climb off their horses even to sleep, with knives this big at their waist, who for some trifle or another mark your face, or worse still, disembowel you and if they get too merry they might slit your throat, butcher you, as they put it. Cruel gauchos that don't set foot in the city, and that it's best not to meet up with in the countryside either by day or by night, the Spaniard says. He treats them like dogs, and in return they obey him like dogs. If he were to ask them for their mother, they would bring her to his bed, the Spaniard says. Two or three years ago one of the ranch hands gave twenty knife wounds to an Englishman who had picked up his sister, and the Englishman's brother came from Córdoba to look for him with some soldiers so as to have him shot to death. Believe me, the Spaniard says, Juan Garay López was opposed. They couldn't take the gaucho away. After much bargaining, they gave the Englishman some cows as recompense. It was that or nothing, or maybe twenty more knife wounds. So the Englishman from Córdoba was forced to accept, the Spaniard says.

Bianco pours him a third little glass of brandy; after casting his inevitable swift glances around the room, the Spaniard drains it in one gulp, wipes his lips with the back of his hand, and in a thoughtful mood strokes his pepper-and-salt beard: they own everything, he says, lowering his voice again, as though the sentence that he has just uttered was the worst of insults or the most dangerous of revelations. That's why they're always fighting with people in Buenos Aires, in Paraguay, Montevideo, Corrientes or Córdoba, he says. On one day certain provinces ally themselves against others, and the next, those who were enemies become allies and fight against the others; and in the middle of the battle, the Spaniard says, they betray each other for a few head of cattle. Land and cattle drive that bunch out of their minds, the Spaniard says, moving his head again in a vague circular motion, to designate the entire region. They slit throats and betray each other for land and cattle, the Spaniard says. Around here it's best to keep your mouth shut and mind your own business, he says, lowering his voice a little. He and his wife mind the inn; they work hard but with God's help they are doing well, they don't meddle in politics, and don't keep company with that sort of people.

A few days later, when the formalities of registering his land are over, when the limits, the location and the exact dimensions of his property have been set down in the official documents of the province, Bianco buys three horses, gathers together a light load of equipment in which he does not neglect to include either a revolver or two or three books, or a little paper and ink, or a carbine, and one morning in autumn, very early, he sets out for the pampas.

He does not come back to the city until the beginning of the following spring. Well, I'll be damned, the Spaniard who owns the inn says to him when he sees him come in the door after six months: we thought you'd never come back. The Spaniard doesn't notice, but the very fine wrinkles that Bianco has around his eyes have become just a little deeper. His long, curly crop of red hair matted together, his brick-colored eyelashes have a metallic consistency, as though the bad weather of so many months had covered them with a very fine copper film. When he goes to bed that night in his room at the inn, it is the first time in six months that his body, a little more dried up, less bulky than before he left, has the experience of contact with a bed. It seems too soft, uncomfortable to Bianco, and his muscles, accustomed to the firm and indifferent resistance of the ground, find it hard to get used to the pliability of the mattress. In the six months since he has disappeared from the city, Bianco has journeyed across the pampas in every direction, avoiding the rare villages and even the isolated cabins or ranch houses, living constantly in the open, rarely climbing down from his horse during the day, indifferent to the rain, to the sun that beats down even in winter, to the wind or the frosts, hunting for his food or buying his provisions in the rather desolate general stores in the desert where the halfbreeds would see him arrive, silent, serious, with his revolver at his waist, mounted on one horse and driving the other two before him or leading them with a long rein alongside or behind his mount. In the six months, he hasn't once slept with a roof over his head and in a bed, he has spoken with almost no one, except for two or three routine exchanges with the owner of a general store or with a horseman passing by in the middle of the pampas, speaking the language without shyness or hesitation now, with a foreign accent even stronger than the one he has even when speaking his mother tongue, providing one could find out exactly what language is his mother tongue. He has attentively observed the soil, the pasturelands, the animals, the sky, watching the constellations fade little by little at dawn, he has paid close attention to the direction and the strength of the winds; hunched over underneath a rainproof cape, almost between the horses' legs, he has waited for the torrential rains that last for two or three days, electrical storms, hailstorms to pass. At times, he has looked like a ghostly presence on the smooth and empty plain, with his three well-selected horses, better than almost all the others that he has come across on the pampas. He has purposely let himself be seen in deserted fields, passed by the same places several times, so as to indicate clearly his presence, his existence, his reality and has gone around the perimeter of his land several times to mark his territory unmistakably and make its boundaries evident to others, he has spent all his days on the pampas in order to reconnoiter it from inside, trying to interiorize it, to make it consubstantial with himself, tending to construct from within himself the perceptions experienced by those born there, those who, like Adam in his view of Paradise, are kneaded from the gray clay that the hoofs of their horses trample underfoot, landowners, ranch hands, Indians, muleteers, carters, cattle rustlers and even fugitives from justice and murderers. So that when at the end of these incessant goings and comings, imperturbable and almost stoic, a week before returning to the city, he climbs out of the saddle and enters a bar in order to hire two or three ranch hands, not only the owner of the place but also the ranch hands, the vagabonds and murderers that are drinking brandy or gin next to the grille that protects the bar counter or at one of the rickety tables, know him, have learned, who knows how, that in spite of his red hair he is not an Englishman, that he owns twenty square leagues south of the Salado River, that doubtless he is trying to place animals in it, and that undoubt-edly he is dismounting from his horse in front of the entrance to the bar so as to offer work to those who are free at the moment. When he leaves, two or three gauchos accompany him, with-drawn, almost timid before this foreigner who rides a horse better than theirs and who rides it with the same agility and skill as they do, and who already appears to know the region as well as they do. It is not the revolver that he is wearing at his waist that impels them to respect him, the revolver that forms part of his attire, like his sombrero or his trousers, and that he seems to be wearing unthinkingly, although something tells them that he would not hesitate a second to use it should that prove neces-sary, no, it is not the revolver, but those many months spent out of doors in all weather and the imperturbability that he has acquired as he endured them or thanks to which he was able to endure them, his having gotten under the skin of the pampas and dug his own tunnels in it like a mole, his having traveled from one end of it to the other unharmed, accepting its laws, without, however, allowing himself to be destroyed by them. What the ranch hands do not know is that what they regard as an initiation, almost an epic feat, to Bianco is simply the result of a calculation, an obligatory period of time that he must get through, now that he has made up his mind to get rich, and in order to do so he knows that he must become intimately acquainted with, and in a certain sense master, the land where he is going to settle and the men who inhabit it. This whole long ride all through the pampas has been no more than an arduous but necessary journey in order to pass from the state in which he finds himself to another much more intense and agree-able one, a mere pretext as well for having at his disposal the necessary leisure to devote himself to refuting the positivists, the servile fodder of matter and scribblers perched atop the supposed lookout posts of the century. What the ranch hands believe that Bianco has done in order to be equal to them, in reality, this transition from one identity to another without lingering in either has been made in order to differentiate himself more clearly from them, and his apprenticeship is no more a desire for fusion than the observations of a hunter concerning the habits of a tiger with the aim of domesticating it or of selling its pelt. The fact remains that when he returns to the city, the cowhands are already working for him even though he hasn't yet let a single animal loose on his land.

Several letters from Garay López are awaiting him in the inn. The first of them is a reply to the one that Bianco had sent him on his arrival, a sort of rather nonsensical narrative satire on Bianco's adventures among the notables, at chocolate parties, at balls and at business meetings, but in the second letter Garay López is surprised that he has not yet gone to visit his family, as he has learned by way of a letter from one of his sisters. In the third missive he shows a certain concern about Bianco's silence, and even allows a note of irritation to show through, a reproachful tone that makes Bianco smile. The last one, in turn, adopts, out of resentment perhaps, that insolent, rather indiscreet tone that Bianco's mysterious origins and his calculated reserve arouse in him. "Cher ami ... dear friend ... caro amico ... I don't know what language to begin this letter in to express to you my anxiety and my perplexity. I know that you cherish mystery, that in your case it is perhaps part and parcel of your profession, but I assure you that your silence of over four months worries me a little, since I have been informed by the keeper of the inn where you were lodging that all your belongings are still piled up in his garret and that since your departure you haven't given the least sign of life. I believe you to be prudent enough not to commit mortal errors, but the harsh knocks of this wild territory can catch you off guard. Please believe me that I ascribe to you the most noble of superiorities, that of the mind, but the equivocal atmosphere to which your reserve lends sustenance disturbs me a little, and I seem to sense in you, behind the serene bust of the thinker, the shadow of the adventurer."

With his pen in his hand, held suspended in the air, the white sheet of paper on the table, Bianco remains motionless, pensive, before deciding on the words with which he will begin his reply, and after a few moments' hesitation, he finally dips the pen in the inkwell. "Caro dottore," he begins in Italian and then goes on, to the end of the letter, and more or less inexplicably, in French. "In one of your letters you reproach me for not yet having visited your family, but it was displeasing to me to do so when certain practical problems had not yet been resolved, out of fear of imposing on your family the task of resolving them. Now that I have the impression of being a local man, I can permit myself to pay a totally disinterested call on them. I should like you to know that I have spent all these months in the country, in the most complete solitude, surviving by hunting, talking to no one, alternating the exercise of pure thought and the accumulation of pragmatic knowledge. Although it was unjustified, I thank you for your apprehensiveness, and on another level, I must tell you that I take the word *adventurer*, which you set down in writing, not without vehemence but with a certain insouciance, in its epic and not its moral connotation."

Finally, a week after having returned from the countryside, Bianco goes to visit Garay López's family – he has himself announced by the messenger boy from the inn, sending off with him so that it precedes him, Garay López's letter of introduction, and from the hands of the same messenger boy he receives, written in a rather laborious feminine hand, an invitation for the next day. A Paraguayan servant girl shows him into the patio, where, beneath a flowering wisteria, through which the sunlight of five in the afternoon filters, Garay López's father and his two sisters, sitting in wicker armchairs, are awaiting him, and the father, with a slightly hesitant air, rises halfway to his feet as he sees him enter.

"My son announced your visit several months ago. Did something go wrong?"

Bianco notes that the man is sincerely trying to be friendly but that something about the situation is bothering him, the fact, perhaps, that Bianco has come to them with a letter of introduction from his older son, something which, Bianco thinks, may cause him complications with the younger one, if it is true that the two brothers detest each other so violently. But there is something more: everything about the man betrays a general malaise, a lack of adaptation to his body or to the world, which is noticeable in his flaccid and changeable face, in the awkward shape of his feet, in the hesitant solicitude he displays toward others, less out of courtesy than out of fear that their initiative, causing them to be overbearing in the expression of their desires, may destroy him. Although he must be some sixty years old at most, he already feels wasted away and lost – something must have cracked in him at some precise moment of his life, perhaps long before the death of his wife, which has been the pretext and not the real cause of the appearance of that devastated air, of that disintegrating will. And the daughters, who must be between twenty-two and twenty-five, huddling in that poisonous shadow, are already beginning, prematurely, to fade. They appear to have set aside all desire, in the name of who knows what principles unknown even to themselves, but ceaselessly spread throughout their entire being by the circulation of humors and the continual renewal of their tissues. They give the impression, not of expecting nothing, but of not wanting to expect anything, full of grayness, even with the approach of the summer that is spreading a warm light amid the wisteria. Bianco, who before coming has told himself that one of Garay López's sisters might be an interesting marriage for a man like himself who plans to get rich, has realized at first sight, just by perceiving them sitting there in their wicker armchairs, that the very idea of such a marriage, or of any marriage for themselves, would never even occur to them, that not only would their minds remain closed, impermeable to a proposal, but that their ears too would close, as resistant to the sound as their understanding is to the meaning of the words.

"No, no misadventures," Bianco says, sitting down in the wicker chair that the man points to.

"We correspond regularly with Antonio. He's not coming this summer. He comes less and less often. Do you like maté? I don't drink it," the man says.

"No, thank you. I've just had one," Bianco says, and on noting his accent, the man asks him:

"Italian?"

"The island of Malta," Bianco says. "Half Italian, half English."

"We arrived here at almost the same time as Christopher Columbus," the man says; and then, feigning a disinterested curiosity: "Your land is right next to ours, isn't that so?"

"Yes," Bianco replies. "That's precisely what I wanted to talk to you about, but that's for some other day. Talking business will bore the ladies."

"If it's about business, you'll have to talk to my younger son. I don't take care of such things any more," the man says. "Are you thinking of growing grain?"

"No," Bianco says. "What interests me for the moment is cattle."

"There are good pasturelands hereabouts," the man says.

Bianco nods. All of a sudden he notes that the man gives a start, very slight, hidden, one might say, and one might also say that he has the involuntary desire to look behind him and that at the same time he is trying his best to repress it, and when

Bianco raises his head and turns his eyes toward the far end of the patio, he understands the reasons for the man's sudden start and for his uneasiness. His younger son has stopped in the doorway that leads to the second patio, some twelve yards away, wearing a collarless shirt, a pair of faded balloon trousers of an indefinable color, and a narrow-brimmed sombrero pushed back a little, his hands in the pockets of his balloon trousers, and his feet bare, his face and his neck almost black, tanned again and again by the sun, slim and muscular, his belly so flat that he gives the impression, undoubtedly illusory, of being slightly stooped over, swaying a little from side to side, contemptuous and mistrustful, like a slightly evil mass of intermittent particles of energy, little igneous projectiles or radiations, his mouth with narrow, tense lips, the nerves, arteries and muscles of his neck standing out, twisted like dark roots, his cruel eyes fixed on Bianco, who, when their eyes meet, smiles faintly in greeting, to which the other replies with a movement of his head, which it is impossible to say whether it is a greeting or an irate rejection, before disappearing as swiftly and silently as he has appeared, into the second patio.

Bianco spends the summer in Buenos Aires. Sometimes, in the early evening, he goes to meet Garay López at the exit of the hospital, and before having dinner, they go for a stroll along the river. One day, Garay López, his voice half ironic and half serious, and at the same time in the tone of one who is offering a veiled warning, stretching his arm out with a melodramatic gesture, points to the water of a milky brown color, and says to him: "Those who came from Europe searching for this river were eaten by Indians." Sometimes, when Garay López is on night duty, Bianco goes to visit him at the hospital and stays to chat with him until dawn is about to break, at the entrance to the hospital, underneath the trees along the sidewalk in chairs with straw seats that a nurse brings out for them as soon as she sees Bianco coming. If they come to get Garay López for some emergency, Garay López leaves his lighted cigar on the doorsill, and Bianco patiently waits for him, sitting in his chair, beneath the dark foliage pierced by moonbeams, watching the fireflies go by, giving off a greenish phosphorescence, like slow, silent and intermittent thoughts. Mistrustful by nature, Bianco confides in Garay López not out of the necessity to confide in someone, but because of the contagion of that immediate, total confidence that Garay López seemingly proffers him, and whose frequent insolent remarks, ironic and veiled, are merely a freedom that he permits himself because of his admiration, indicating precisely by way of that insolence that his admiration also encompasses Bianco's obscure past, whose inavowable nature Garay López wishes to hint that he is not unaware of. Bianco, more or less outraged in the beginning, is starting to become accustomed to it, in the first place because to admit to outrage would be to concede that he understands the allusion, and secondly because he sees in that insolence the proof of Garay López's total acceptance of him. And as early as that summer, the salutations "Cher ami" and "Caro dottore" that they exchange in their letters and, always with an ironic nuance, in their conversations, and above all in their disagreements, are somewhat more than empty formulas or instinctive reflexes.

And the following autumn, he writes to Garay López beneath the orange trees of the inn: "Your uncle the governor is an excellent businessman. Thanks to him I have been able to secure my first thousand head of cattle. My cowhands are already taking care of them for me, and I even have an overseer. It is true that I don't have a house and am living at the inn, but as I understand it, in my new status as a cattle rancher, a house is the thing I need least." In December, Garay López comes to the city: "This is the first Christmas that I've spent *en famille* for ten years," he explains to Bianco, and Bianco, with that quick smile that seems bitter because of the shape of his lips, remarks:

"If I understand your theatrical allegory rightly, for you, that day which you come to celebrate with your family really has no reason to be a cause for celebration, since nobody was born on that day."

"Don't attribute any importance to my actions, cher ami. Only to my writings," Garay López replies. Every so often, they eat at the inn, or go horseback riding in the country. Juan, the brother, has always gone to the ranch as soon as Garay López announced his arrival. And one hot afternoon, when after having ridden for hours they halt at a pond so as to water their horses, they see a group of men on horseback approaching the water at a slow trot, almost a walk, from the west, and as it is only all of a sudden that they become aware of their arrival, the group of horsemen seem like an apparition standing out against the reddish sun as it goes down. On the pampas, everything seems to be bigger than it really is, more compact, more bounded by its precise outline, but that excess of reality in the empty expanse, that impressive presence floating in the void, always borders on a mirage, and because it achieves its effect so frequently, this works toward its own ruin.

"It's Juan, with his gauchos. Look, Bianco, look, they're like animals," Garay López murmurs, pulling discreetly on his shirt sleeve. "He deprived me of a mother when he was born."

Bianco perceives the horror in Garay López's expression, a hatred in which discouragement and sadness are also present, and he must make an effort, he who since he was fifteen, in the outlying districts of a city that overlooks the Mediterranean, has long ago learned to control his emotions, so that in his face which the sun of the pampas does not succeed in darkening, there is no sign of the fascination aroused in him by those seven or eight horsemen who are advancing very slowly toward the opposite bank of the pond and halt there so as to water their horses, without casting a single glance their way. The violet surface of the pond, so smooth and luminous, affects the outlines of the horsemen, which seem to glitter. In the middle of them, the brother, shorter than the cowhands, a little hunched over the neck of his horse as it leans down toward the water, looks into empty space, his head to one side, protected by the strict and perhaps slightly embarrassed silence of the cowhands who have no doubt recognized Garay López, those cowhands who, as Garay López has told him more than once, used to play with him at the ranch and at night would accompany him on horseback to the entrances to the city. With difficulty, Bianco represses his astonished respect for that sort of power that emanates from the group, he sees them as exterior, all of a piece, strangers to pity and hesitation, identical to the spirit that moves them, capable of fidelity and of violence, although, like pumas and snakes, violence and fidelity mean nothing to them. After a few minutes, as though they had been alone on the pampas over which night is already falling, they turn their horses around, which splash for a moment at the water's edge, and go off at a brisk trot first, and then at a gallop to the spot on the pampas where they first made their appearance.

A few days later, shortly before returning to Buenos Aires, Garay López suggests to Bianco that, since the pampas seems to him the most suitable place for devoting himself entirely to thought, he build himself a cabin in the middle of the countryside, far from the city, in which to retire and concentrate. Just as happens every time that an idea seems exactly right to him, Bianco remains motionless and lost in thought for a moment, and then finally agrees. An old ranch hand of the Garay Lópezes builds it for him. One morning, they arrive at the chosen site, and the old man, who has brought with him a whole bunch of different-sized stakes without Bianco's knowing where they came from or how, has already driven the four main ones marking the four angles of the cabin and has begun to mix mud and dung in a puddle of water. Two days later, he puts on the straw roof and respectfully bids him and Garay López goodbye, without having ever once opened his mouth, and when Bianco tries to give him some banknotes, the old man, before taking them, gazes questioningly at Garay López, who approves with a nod of his head.

"You'll either work out your system here, or else nowhere," Garay López says to him from the back of his horse, before going off to the city and then to Buenos Aires the following day.

Bianco watches the old man go off, and Garay López as well, a compact mass at first, and then a mirage that finally dissolves on the pampas. The first house he has is that brand-new, precarious cabin, deliberately empty and humble, so as to bring forth thought from him, from his deserted and silent surroundings, like ice-cold and muffled blows, in its dual expression as pure and as pragmatic reflections. To tell the truth, he is too lenient a judge of himself, and since the night in Paris, almost without being conscious of it, there mingle within him, perhaps even until his death, blindness about himself, deeply buried humiliation that still perturbs him, with its violent, mortal jolts, and resentment. By dint of wanting to confuse everyone as to his origins, he is ending up by confusing his origins himself, and what is opaque and hazy for everyone else is now that way for himself as well, so that the successive masks that he has been wearing from his uncertain beginnings, in an uncertain place – he no longer knows quite which – the masks of Valletta, of the Orient, of London, of Prussia, of Paris, of Buenos Aires press, viscously, against his face, and deform it, efface it, turn it into mere perishable and residual material, transform his very own self into the living argument of those whom he detests, of those who, ripping off his mask in Paris, thinking that they would discover his true face, left in its place a black hole, that he is little by little filling up with property rights, with cattle, with this cabin in whose doorway he is now observing how Garay López, posting up and down on his horse, is growing smaller and smaller on the horizon until he disappears completely.

And it will also be from the cabin that, sitting in the sun the following spring, in the flowing, very careful, and rather slow handwriting of someone who has perhaps learned to write late in life, he will compose, with a new pleasure, unknown to him or probably now forgotten at the age of forty-three, a letter to Garay López:

"My talent for business is confirmed with each passing day. But raising cattle isn't enough for me. The cattle ranchers in this region, as you know better than I, caro dottore, live in another century and there are numerous problems that stem from sharing a space. I can't say that there are problems with your family: after being here for three years, I have been unable to have a single conversation with your brother. I feel a strong inclination to strike out in other directions, agriculture, for just one, and commerce in general, and later on, why not, importing and industry. I know that in Europe, for example, they are enclosing their fields with wire fences, so as to clearly mark the limits of their property, keep their cattle where they belong and content at one and the same time cattle raisers and farmers. Some day perhaps we'll see these fields here a little more civilized.

"But I'm taking a roundabout way so as not to tell you the real news. Did you know that I'm having a house built? I want it to be a big one, with two patios, many rooms, a good-looking foyer and a bit of marble in the entryway. At first I thought of building it several floors high, as you have no doubt seen is becoming the fashion in Buenos Aires, but I finally decided to follow the local model. And now comes the real news: I have met a young person, the daughter of Italian immigrants, although she herself was born here in your city, so we can consider her as belonging to the same province as you do. I have been visiting the family regularly for three or four months now, and if I dare speak with her father, it's because it seemed to me that I have perceived in certain of the daughter's attitudes that I am not wholly a matter of indifference to her. When you meet her, you will see that I am not exaggerating when I tell you that she is a great beauty. And her father has given me her hand without hesitation. However, we have decided to wait for a while before getting married, since Gina – that is the name of the adorable child – needs, according to her mother, a little preparation for marriage, since she has just turned sixteen."

With his eyes half-closed, not moving, in his shirt sleeves, Bianco is sitting in the center of the living room in a near semi-darkness assailed by the luminous rays of the springtime afternoon filtering in everywhere, the slats of the blinds, the fanlight of the door opening onto the foyer, the joints of windows and doors, the keyholes of locks; a silence that seems premeditated reigns in the house and Bianco's self-absorption and immobility are so thoroughgoing that when the wheels of a cart and the hoofs of the horse that is pulling it, not to mention the rhythmical hitting of shafts and harnesses against each other, pass by on the street of beaten earth in front of the house and head off for some other part of the city, Bianco not only does not change position, but he doesn't even hear the noise, and more than a minute probably goes by before, slowly and gently shaking his head, as though he were coming out of a fainting spell or a dream, prudently opening his eyes, separating his soft, joined hands that have dropped together onto his abdomen, he rises to his feet, and with a resolute and natural pace, he opens the door and goes out onto the porch that overlooks the first patio. On the other side of the patio, on the porch opposite, Gina, sitting in a wicker armchair alongside the door of the bedroom, is leaning her elbows on a little varnished wicker table, and with her eyes closed, is holding her head in her two hands, her thumbs underneath her jaw and her other fingers resting on her temples, and although on closing the door behind him Bianco has made a little noise, Gina, deep in thought and with a serious look on her face, does not change position, and when Bianco crosses the sunny patio and plants himself in front of her, next to the little wicker table, he still has to wait a few seconds more before Gina, letting her hands fall back onto the table, one on each side of the light blue cardboard rectangle with rounded corners placed on top of it, raises her head, opening her eyes wide as she contemplates him with a grave, questioning look.

"A bunch of grapes," Bianco says.

Gina shakes her head, pressing her lips together slightly.

"Banana," she says. And turning the light blue rectangle over, with her dark, delicate, rather bony hand, she shows him the stylized sketch of the glaringly yellow banana, standing out clearly on a diagonal, against an incontestable pink background.

Slowly, irrelevantly, Bianco moves his head in turn, but in an affirmative nod, to demonstrate that his new failure is already recorded in his anticipations, and then, indifferent to the gentle, steady spring sunshine that is flowing impalpably over the patio, he scrutinizes Gina's oval face, crowned by her coal-black hair, caught up in a topknot at the apex of her head. Her long matte neck emerges from her light, flower print dress, and the skin of her throat quivers a little as she appears to swallow something, a few drops of saliva perhaps, or some humor that is circulating, autonomous and secret, through the internal folds of her body, sheltered from the light of this October afternoon. But her big wide-open eyes do not evade the insistent look that is questioning them.

"Third failure in a row," Bianco says.

"Shall we try again?" Gina suggests.

"Not today," Bianco says, as his gaze continues to study Gina's face.

For some time, that face has been an unknown, labyrinthine territory to him, in which he seeks, with well-concealed anxiety, signs, however small they may be, that will permit him to orient himself, to know something about the internal region that lives and stirs behind that territory, the spring of images and of emotions into which he cannot succeed in projecting himself, but where he would like to immerse himself as in deep water, in order to examine, one by one, resolutely and minutely, the living masses teeming in confusion at the bottom. But the smoothness of her skin, the simplicity of her gaze, that withstands his, allow nothing to pass outside, and Bianco thinks that that simplicity, so diaphanous and so natural, could be the proof, not of the innocence that it suggests, but of a greater deviation, of such an identification with perversity, that the very notion of perversion is alien to the untamed energy of her desires. So, now, for the first time, Bianco asks himself if Gina is not setting traps for him during their experiments in telepathic communication: since it is Sunday, taking advantage of the fact that all the maids are gone for the day, they have decided to try to communicate mentally ever since that morning, and the three experiments that they have performed, two after breakfast and the one that they have just finished have failed, like all the others that they have attempted since they got married and moved into the house, the year before. This is the first time that Bianco has had this suspicion. The last experiment which they tried, and which was also a failure, took place at the end of August, the night he came back from the country, as a matter of fact, and found her puffing on a cigar, with an expression of intense pleasure, in the company of Garay López, who was saying something to her in a low voice with a wicked smile on his face, but not even that time, despite his feeling upset, or perhaps for that very reason, did it occur to him that Gina might deliberately fool him during their sessions of telepathic communication.

"Are you certain you concentrated hard enough?" Bianco says.

"I followed all your instructions," Gina says, her face clouding over a little.

"Come on, don't take offense," Bianco says, gently placing his hand on her shoulder and giving her a little shake, with forced joviality.

"Maybe it's my fault," Gina says.

"In any event, that's enough for today," Bianco says.

Gina gets to her feet, and from the pocket of her flower print dress, takes out the other two images and leaves them next to the stylized design of the exaggeratedly yellow banana standing out in slight relief against the pink background, which is lying on the table. Bianco glances fleetingly at the three cards and then, turning around, begins to contemplate the sunny patio, with no expression in particular on his face. Gina takes a few steps and stands next to him.

Even if they had tried, they would not have succeeded in being as different from each other as they are in the clear, gentle sunlight of the first day of October: at least a head taller than Bianco, supple and moving about easily, full of firm, full roundnesses, but svelte and energetic inside her short-sleeved flower print dress that clings to her bosom and her hips and flares out in a whirl of motley colors down to her ankles, Gina is like an expanding force, flexible, compact, and at the age of nineteen there is not the slightest shadow of the matron that she will doubtless be later on, when her purely feminine side begins to predominate, because the energy that emanates from her now is independent of her sex, almost, one could say, of her person, so that it blends with the impersonal and abstract radiance of that beauty which, even though it penetrates us by means of our senses, is grasped, in its felicitous equations, in an instantaneous operation, by means of our intelligence; a beauty that is made

up of contradictions and impatiences, of sudden and shortlived
fits of rage and of childish abandon, of loquacity and of unjustified silences, of ignorance of its own existence and even of the
very notion of beauty, consisting of exteriority, so as to attain at
certain moments, despite so many contradictions, a sort of simplicity, like that of a green leaf, for instance, or that of an egg,
which, though constituted of so many elements capable of
developing an infinitely intricate complexity, shows itself in its
simplest form, concentrating its entire substance in two colors –
white and yellow – so pure that it ends up transforming itself,
through its very simplicity, into the emblem of its multiplicity.
Bianco, at her side, stocky, almost without a neck, his brick-
colored hair, curly and wiry, his white skin that the sun of the
pampas does not manage to darken, the very fine little wrinkles
that furrow his puerile face, enveloped in his own mysteries
which he himself has built into a fortress, entrenched within the
complicated construction of his calculations, in his incessant
rumination on his secrets, with his gaudy attire in the choice of
which affectation plays no part whatsoever, occupied in present-
ing to the outside world an imperturbable image and managing
to do so, encrusted in the pampas, ramifying, without pause and
with no possible error, his subterranean tunnels, feeling for the
first time, and endeavoring to conceal it at all costs, that that
supple, nameless creature moving at his side, who has breathed in
bed, naked, next to him every night for a year now, is the real
trap into which he has fallen, and that in relation to it, the trap
that the positivists laid for him so long ago in Paris is an innocent
practical joke thought up by a bunch of students. The Bianco
machine has the feeling that a foreign body, a screw, a wrench, a
roll of rusty wire, has fallen, out of carelessness, amid the gears
and pulleys and that the moment is close at hand when the
mechanism will jam, stop working, explode. Gina puts her arm
around his shoulder, and draws him a little closer to her.

"We're going to succeed soon," she says.

Bianco looks at her gratefully, but Gina, as though she had already forgotten what she has just said, is contemplating the blue sky that is opening up above the patio paved in mosaic tiles, a rectangle without a single cloud, from which the sun is absent, but from which the spring light seems to flow.

"We should have gone to eat with my family," she says. "I never see them."

"They came here to lunch last Sunday," Bianco says, vaguely irritated by Gina's inconsistency.

"That's true," Gina says.

And letting go of him, as though she had been leaning against a tree or a pillar, she turns around and goes into the bedroom. Feeling somewhat humiliated, Bianco halts in hesitation, and then, with the same abruptness with which Gina has gone into the bedroom, he heads for the street door and sits down on the marble doorstep, staring at the sidewalk. The shadow of two chinaberry trees, at the edge of the ditch, protects him from the sun. The street is deserted, and to tell the truth, no more than three or four houses have been built on the entire block; everything else is vacant lots, patios and gardens. Unlike traditional families, who live in clusters of colonial houses in the south of the city, Bianco has decided to build his house in the northern section, near the river, almost in open countryside, and has bought several plots of municipal land, thinking that, with two or three rich immigrants who will have their little mansions built there, the value of the plots of land will go up in just a few years. But he has also bought a house in the southern section of the city, and is having it modernized little by little by his father-in-law, who is a mason, so as to show that if he doesn't live in the south of the city it isn't because his means will not permit him to do so, and that if he has decided to settle in the northern section, it is so as to set the example of a new style of life.

Thoughts occur to him, unexpected and swift, like tiny, repetitive, obstinate flashes. Memories that persist in coming back to him, fragmentary and nearly forgotten images that begin to take on a new, unforeseen, and naturally irrefutable meaning, rush around inside him all at the same time, and Bianco tries, in vain, to put them in order, to crush his humiliation and his fury with feeble, ridiculous shovelfuls of appeals to order and calm, convinced as he is now that Gina, ever since they began their exercises in telepathic communication, is deliberately lying to him, and with pitiless cruelty as well, with the aim of confusing him, of making him lose his way, of weakening his powers. And to Bianco this conviction is far more humiliating inasmuch as he has counted on precisely those powers to seduce her, fascinate her, make himself admired by her and dominate her. Before the wedding, when they found themselves alone together, Bianco used to talk about his powers and Gina seemed to listen to him with interest, with passion at times, and she had told him that she would like to put her own powers to the test – Bianco lets his gaze wander about the deserted street, the sundrenched vacant lots, the gardens in which spring has made the bougainvilleas, the dahlias, the snapdragons and the calla lilies flower, the uneven sidewalks, of beaten earth or of brick, apart from his own, of gray mosaic tiles, the weeds that grow not only in the vacant lots but also in the gutters, along the edges of the sidewalks, on the cornices of the houses. "For a long time, all this will be countryside still, they call them cities, but they're still countryside," he thinks, distracting himself for a moment from his humiliation with one of those pragmatic automatisms that assail him in the middle of his most violent emotions or his most abstract reflections, and rising to his feet, he goes back inside the house again. When he has gone through the foyer and emerges onto the patio, his gaze is directed toward the door of the bedroom, which has been left ajar, showing a vertical strip of semidarkness and he heads for it, but halfway there he changes his mind and turns around facing the back patio. Unlike the first one, it is not tiled, but divided into different sections, a pleasure garden, a vegetable garden, a henhouse, and at the very back a stable and a corral for the horses. When they see him appear, three or four horses that are idly chewing grass raise their heads, cast an indifferent glance, and lower them again.

Bothered, without knowing why, Bianco directs a glance full of hatred at them in return, and unable to tolerate their presence, turns around and goes back to the first patio. Through the half-open door, the strip of semidarkness coming from the bedroom makes silent, insistent signs at him, and it seems to him that he perceives a strange atmosphere, of imminent danger, coming from inside. For a few seconds, he is convinced that Gina is spying on him from behind the door, following, with contained perverseness, his irrational and hesitant goings and comings from one patio to the other. But almost immediately, he experiences a sort of sudden tiredness or discouragement – if she is innocent of all this and is asleep, humiliation and fury are useless and if she is lying and spying on him, they are also useless, he thinks – and heads once more toward the outside door. In the foyer, a new feeling of tiredness and discouragement, appertaining to another object, again assails him, and he stands motionless in the semidarkness, unable to decide to open the street door, out of fear that the view of the deserted street, peaceful and sunny, will awaken in him the same inexplicable desperation foreseen by his imagination. She herself asked me to tell her about my powers, he thinks bitterly, without letting go of the door handle, and now I discover that during the exercises in telepathic communication she is using who knows what tricks so as to confuse me.

"And she is succeeding," he murmurs, in Italian.

Smiling to himself, in such a way that the bitter set of his lips, through a melodramatic exaggeration of his misery, becomes just a little more bitter than usual, Bianco shakes his head, wipes his free hand across his forehead, and turns the door handle. He has expected to receive the street full in the face, like a slap, but it is the same street as always, peaceful, on the edge of the open countryside, where there are more vacant lots, corrals and gardens than houses, and even better than serene, it is welcoming on this spring afternoon. His venom, which has never ceased mounting inside him, does not pour outward, and for a few seconds the warm, quiet street holds back a bit the stampede of his emotions, but, amazed at the strangeness of the situation, Bianco grows impatient when he fails to find in the brilliant foliage of the trees and in the calm of the sandy street any reasons to make his bitterness grow, as though the street, trying to pacify him with its tranquility, had made itself Gina's accomplice. And also because he experiences the paradoxical desire, more or less against nature, to go to the limit of his fury, allowing it to pour out so as to force the outside to reveal itself in this way, to come out into the open, and because it seems to him that fury and humiliation, rather than the consequence, are the proof that what he suspects about Gina is true. He therefore goes back inside the house. He crosses the foyer and emerges in the first patio: the door of the bedroom is still ajar, and the vertical strip of semidarkness exudes ridicule, fear, danger: Bianco contemplates it, and must contain the impulse leading him toward the bedroom: if she is spying on me, he thinks, I don't have to go inside; perhaps she is waiting behind the door for me to do so; it would be like surrendering. And slowly, making a false show of calm, putting his hands in the pockets of his trousers, looking all about, the porches, the sky, the door of the kitchen to his left, on the porch opposite the bedroom, he heads for the back patio. Once again, without knowing why, the horses that are grazing and that raise their heads without any agitation, on seeing him enter the patio, fill him with chagrin and with hatred. I must look into this more carefully, he thinks, and heading down the brick walk that goes through the flower-beds and leads to the corral, he stops alongside the barrier of horizontal tree trunks that separates him from the horses. The animals shiver a little, without conviction, on principle almost, and then calm down. Bianco observes them for a moment, perplexed because of his own feelings, convinced that, owing to an overwhelmingly dizzying association of ideas, or perhaps owing to an excess of emotions, he is attributing to the horses, neutral if not innocent, the origin of his confusion and his bitterness. But the hatred persists, and even increases when his eyes run over the brilliant coats, the tense muscles, the horses' compact mass of flesh, traversed by pulses, by shudders, by palpitations. Material that is bought and sold, he thinks, with scorn, but for a fraction of a second he feels inferior to them, humiliated by the mere massive, obscure, living presence of the animals.

"Easy, Bianco," he says to himself, aloud and in Italian, with a sarcastic murmur and a short little laugh quickly broken off.

Incapable of remaining quietly in one place for more than a few minutes, Bianco turns around and begins to go back down the brick walk, among the flower-beds, heading for the first patio. And when he has taken three or four steps, slow and resolute, the memory comes back to him, perfectly clear and all of a piece, and he then understands the cause of his hatred. The image, the details are so sharply focused, that as he continues to recall them, swift and successive, he experiences a sensation of utter certainty, of strength, a sort of contradictory euphoria inasmuch as, instead of banishing his suspicions, that buried memory comes to mind again, rather, to confirm them and to give a meaning to many scattered and heterogeneous facts that float within him like the remains of a shipwreck on the surface

of dark water: one afternoon, several years earlier, also right at
the height of spring, having arrived at Gina's without announcing
his visit beforehand, so as to speak to his future father-in-law
about the house in the south of the city that he is about to buy
and that he would like his future father-in-law to look at with
his eyes of a professional so as to know exactly how much time
it is going to take to get it back into shape. It is also siesta time
and Bianco raps softly on the door, for fear that his future in-
laws are sleeping – until the day of the wedding, he can't be sure
that they won't change their minds about their daughter, and
Bianco would rather not put them out in any way. He knocks
several times, and since nobody answers, he takes a few steps
down the beaten earth sidewalk, hesitating to enter the house by
a side door that leads directly to the back of the property, where
the vegetable garden, the corral and the henhouse are located.
Perhaps they've eaten in the patio, in the shade of the trees, he
thinks, since the weather is fine, and the old man hasn't yet gone
back to work that afternoon. So that, a bit hesitant, yet at the
same time experiencing that unexplained and slightly fearful
feeling of omnipotence that arises when one begins to explore a
house in the absence of its inhabitants, Bianco passes through
the side door and walks along the wide path, covered with grass
and little red, white and violet verbenas, which leads to the very
back of the property. In the beginning, Bianco doesn't hear a
single sound, either from the house, or from the back patio,
or the street – not a single sound except for the crackling noise
of his shoes brushing against the grass, which, without quite
knowing why, perhaps because his intrusion also makes him feel
a little bit guilty, he tries to muffle. But then, little by little, he
begins to hear, intermittently, a commotion from the horses, a
sound of nervous, muted hoofbeats, ceaselessly pounding in
disorder against the bare ground, and a few brief, hoarse, intermittent neighs, more like bellowing, but hesitant, concentrated,

as though the animal emitting them, devoting its entire being to an action that it is unable to carry through as it wishes, had grown impatient, and were abstractedly emitting those fragmentary and nervous protests. Finally, Bianco reaches the back patio, and through the pear, the plum and the peach trees in flower, his eyes are attracted toward the far end of the property, in the direction of the corral from which the irregular, muted sound of the hoofbeats and the irritated, broken bellowings of the horse seem to be coming.

He soon realizes the cause of the din. In the corral, a horse, at the peak of excitement, is trying to mount a mare which, out of indecision, caprice or discomfort, neither yielding nor fleeing, accepts the act and evades it at the same time. The horse's enormous rod, of a bluish pink, lubricated by his growing excitement, hangs down, oblique and rigid, like a varnished stick, between his hind legs, and sways back and forth, hard and heavy, because of his constant movements as, leaning on his hind legs, he tries to hold himself upright with his front legs on the back of the mare, which remains quietly in place and merely shakes her hind quarters a little at the very moment that the horse, after feeling around the mare's open slit with his rod, gets ready to penetrate her, so that, without knowing whether she is trying to collaborate with him or escape from him, with each movement of her rump the mare keeps him from penetrating her, this being the cause of the nervous and annoyed bellowings of the horse and his unruly and rather clumsy stamping on the ground of the corral. A faint smile shows on Bianco's face, and his brick-colored eyebrows arch slightly as his lips begin to move, reproducing, through the twisting of his mouth and the extreme mobility of his forehead, of his eyebrows, and of his gaze, the efforts of the horse to attain his objective, until, all of a sudden, a detail that had escaped Bianco in the beginning, abruptly draws him out of his enthusiastic concentration: a patch of red, to one side of the corral, causes him to turn his head and discover Gina who, leaning back against a tree, clad in a red house dress, is contemplating, from just a few meters away from the corral, the same scene. Bianco gives a start, shudders, and begins to feel unbearable palpitations in the back of his neck and in his back, between the shoulder blades. Moving forward a little, without making any noise, he loses interest in the horses and concentrates all his attention on Gina's expression; she for her part has been so absorbed in observing the scene that she has not perceived his arrival. Searching for certain emotions, he is unsure of exactly which ones, Bianco studies lingeringly, almost anxiously, Gina's face, but her motionless, concentrated and regular profile allows nothing to appear on the outside, except for an engrossed gravity, a calm, almost apathetic interest, her head bent forward a little, so that her back is no longer even leaning against the tree. But lowering his eyes, Bianco notes the attitude of her right arm, enveloped in the red sleeve of her dress, from which her matte hand, long and delicate, emerges, and Bianco notes that at the end of her arm, stretching slightly backwards, Gina's delicate fingers, the nails filed to a point, forgotten at the outer end of her body, are scratching and clawing the cracked bark of the tree, trying to pull off a piece of it, with a rather fierce persistence, as though all the emotion that Bianco was expecting to find in her face had already descended along her body and was being discharged by way of her sharp-edged oval nails. Bianco is unable to determine whether the emotion that the fingers are expressing is desire, perturbation, or anxiety, for her smooth but deeply concentrating face is serene, neutral, free of any outer agitation, and in order to find out, he comes closer, deliberately making a loud scraping noise with his shoes, as though he were wiping the soles of them on the grass, so as to attract Gina's attention, and by startling her, draw her out of her state of absorption. But, unexpectedly, Gina is the one who surprises him. When she hears the soles of his shoes on the grass, she turns around, and guilelessly, without giving the slightest start, without making any comment, turns toward him and shakes his hand. Bianco searches for some emotion in her face, but her huge dark eyes, open wide, look at him frankly with discreet pleasure, with direct and relaxed sociability. Behind Gina, the horse continues his fruitless attempts, producing the same dull stamping on the ground of the corral, and his constant but broken bellowings, without Gina's face betraying the least sign that she has noticed anything, or that, if she has seen something, what she has seen has produced the least effect on her. With self-possession like that, Bianco thinks in amazement, it wouldn't surprise me if this youngster seventeen years old has exceptional powers that we may some day be able to put to use, but at the same time another thought, more deeply hidden, which does not reach the surface of his mind but which as he is thinking about the other subject manifests itself as an indefinable malaise and which now that he is walking down the brick walk toward the front patio, takes on its full meaning; an unbearable notion, to tell the truth, poisons his admiration for Gina's self-composure and her control over her emotions: the thought that if Gina shows no emotion it is because she feels nothing, not out of lack of energy or insensitivity, but because what the horses are doing a few meters away from her, in the corral, bellowing and stirring up the sandy ground of the corral with their hind legs, is consubstantial with her, forming a single essence with her, and at this moment she is the pair of horses struggling, blindly, in a chaos of flesh gorged with blood. Between her and the horses there is no distance, Bianco thinks, leaving the brick walk behind and entering the front patio.

Halting on the porch, he looks at the half-open door of the bedroom, the strip of vertical semidarkness that attracts and repels him at the same time, and after hesitating for a few seconds, trying to repress waves of discouragement and fury, he crosses the sunny patio and abruptly pushing the door open, goes into the bedroom: Gina is lying face upward in the bed, placid, her eyes open, the palm of one hand resting gently on her forehead; her eyes turn a little way toward the door, but the rest of her body remains motionless.

"What's wrong?" she says, in a tone of voice more affirmative than interrogative, in order to show that she perceives Bianco's inner agitation on his face. And immediately, with slightly childish naïveté, she pats the empty part of the bed with her other hand, to indicate to Bianco that he should come lie down beside her.

Bianco doesn't move.

"It must be my fault," Gina says. "Perhaps I don't rightly understand what it's necessary to do in order to concentrate."

"No, no," Bianco says. "No."

"We can start again whenever you like," Gina says. Sitting up part way in bed, she watches him intently. "It's something more, I think. Have you been drinking cognac?"

Bianco shakes his head. Gina's puerile explanations for his agitation, that he is just now beginning to control, tug at him from opposite directions, dividing him, since at times they appear to be a proof of her sincerity, and at times they give him the impression that they are a new way of involving him in doubt and uncertainty, not to mention the apprehension that if they are really sincere, such explanations would make Gina a banal and quite uninteresting person. But Gina's physical presence calms him down: ever since he found her smoking a cigar, in complete intimacy, with Garay López, he has begun to realize that he will never have the courage necessary to ask her directly what it is that he wants to know so badly. Also because he is convinced, without ever having considered the problem, that he has no way of inducing Gina to tell him the truth, that Gina would be capable of denying to the very end, with conviction and obstinacy, not only out of fear or hypocrisy, but also possessed of the most unshakeable belief that, even though she has committed the worst possible betrayals, she has nothing to confess. But there is an even greater obstacle to making the truth come out in some other way than by forcing it, through subterfuges and complicated stratagems, to reveal itself: ever since he has known Gina something in Bianco whispers constantly, accompanying his acts by day and by night, that theirs is an alliance against nature and that each step he takes exposes him a little more every day to the blind gale of an unknown force, a danger forgotten in forty years of complex machinations destined to manipulate, with contempt and complete freedom, the adverse matter of the world. This secret intuition has led him to consider union with Gina as a challenge, a struggle against that force that Bianco conceives of as a trap set for him by matter, a trap of which his own sentiments toward Gina are the prolongations or the most subtle meshes. If he can bend Gina to his will, it is the whole of matter which must submit to him, obey him, and what others would call pride or arrogance, Bianco regards as lucidity, watchfulness, vigilance of the mind in the face of the perishable and archaic disorders of dull flesh left to itself. That battle is even more superhuman since Bianco carries it on in secret, obliged to make the supplementary effort of ensuring that not a single one of its episodes appears on the outside, convinced that, in order to free matter from the vice in which it struggles he must present to the world an air of equanimity, of imperturbability, a reassuring fiction, the smooth surface of his own image, distributed in compact and well-defined volumes, without harsh sounds or abrupt transitions, like a daguerreotype.

"I feel guilty," Gina says.

"There's no reason to," Bianco says, and to reassure her, rests, with no intention of remaining there very long, his buttocks on the edge of the bed.

Gina stretches her hand out to seize his plump white fingers, covered on the back with a sparse reddish down, but pretending not to have noticed Gina's movement, Bianco withdraws his hand and places it along with the other against his belly. Unaware that Bianco has purposely withdrawn his hand, Gina lets hers fall back on the green and white stripes of the bed-spread.

"It's not worth worrying about. I'm a little tired, that's all," Bianco says, and getting to his feet, leaves the bedroom and goes to sit in the wicker armchair by the door.

The first time he saw Gina was in the patio of the inn. Bianco was sitting underneath the trees, after lunch, enjoying the contrast between the cool shadow of the trees and the warm air everywhere else around, drinking a glass of lemonade with the Spaniard, for whom Bianco's company had become indispensable, in particular ever since Bianco had made him a loan, at a reasonable rate of interest, to be used to add rooms to the inn, since business seemed to be going well, because of the travelers, the majority of them foreigners – Englishmen, Frenchmen, Spaniards, Italians – who passed through the city on business, for political reasons, or out of sheer curiosity. The Spaniard was waiting for Cosme, Gina's father, to discuss, in fact, the construction of the new rooms, when Bianco noticed the flower print dress, of simple, light fabric, which swirled about her shoes when her feet moved forward, advancing amid the trees toward the far end of the patio; for a few seconds, before raising his eyes, Bianco kept them riveted on the undulation of the hem which, stirring the flowered fabric, produced, above her little white shoes, an agitated strip of fluted folds, of quiverings, of movements back and forth which gave the flowers of the cloth fleeting appearances, multicolored and capricious, as though instead of being a mere print fabric, it was an effervescence of live things subjected to multiple transformations. And when he raised his head and saw the oval face, surmounted by a modest, precariously balanced little white straw hat, he could see that, even without the hat and the topknot on which it was resting, the young girl was taller than her father, and in addition, more than her father, who was approaching, a bit intimidated, with his hat in his hand, she was in the world without any type of scruples, fear, or arrogance, contemporary at every instant with her being, and a stranger both to doubt and to vanity. More than her physical beauty, which did not fail to excite Bianco at that very moment, it was that intimacy with the world, serene, straightforward, natural, that attracted his attention. The father stood conversing for a moment with the Spaniard, who offered them a glass of lemonade that they drank without sitting down, and Bianco, becoming uninterested in the conversation, cast furtive glances at Gina that she appeared not to notice. And when the father and daughter left after a while, Bianco let the Spaniard talk for a long time about his plan for enlarging the inn, even asking him for many details, so as to postpone for as long as possible the question that he had been thinking of asking from the moment that Gina had appeared in the patio, and finally he interrupted him:

"Is he a good mason?"

"He's more than a mason," the Spaniard said. "He's a building contractor."

"To tell the truth," Bianco said, "one is very comfortable in your establishment, but I think the time has come to have my own house."

"A pity," the Spaniard said, with enigmatic courtesy.

At the very moment that Gina and her father were going off, Bianco was already thinking: I must let a couple of months at least go by and then, for another couple of months, speak only of the house, and then for a couple of months after that act in such a way as to make the family see the relation that exists between Gina and the house, that a young lady of good family like Gina is unthinkable without a house like the one that I'm planning to build, but that the house without Gina for a man of my age, who has been knocking about the world for such a long time, is a superfluous object.

The proof that his plans were calculated down to the last millimeter is that before having spoken with Gina's father, he wrote to Garay López, as though it were a *fait accompli*, extracting from the inevitable nature of his predictions a supplementary satisfaction. When he received Garay López's reply congratulating him – a quite rapid reply, if a bit ironic – as yet he had no reason for receiving those felicitations, since officially he had not declared himself as a serious suitor, and the family knew nothing about the matter, but Bianco did not have the slightest doubt that reality, like a sheet of wallpaper, was merely waiting for him to come to fold it in four and put it in the pocket of his waistcoat. And he was not mistaken: as he had calculated almost instantaneously the moment that he saw her for the first time, six months later Gina was his fiancée in the same way that the house – which had been an abstract scheme, an imaginary object, just as in a game of chess a move which has no value in itself and is made only in order to win the match later – was now under construction. In all this, only one thing worried him; it was obvious that the family was more than satisfied by the choice of Bianco, and that a good marriage for the daughter, in view of her beauty and her education, must have seemed to them something pertinent and necessary, inherent in the very logic of things, but what left Bianco perplexed, thereby giving proof of a certain contradiction in him, was that that immediate acceptance was also shared by Gina, without any sort of emotional effusion, any sign whatsoever, either positive or negative, of her feelings, to the point that Bianco, in the beginning, wondered more than once, and all the time later on, if that acceptance was not, rather, indifference – not even resignation, but indifference, since in resignation there is something somber and burned out that was totally absent in Gina. Whereas the family's motives were transparent, Gina's escaped him. At first, he would go to see her once a week, on Sunday afternoons, and every so often he was invited to dinner. As time went by, his visits became more frequent and fairly often the two of them were left alone for some time in the living room, or underneath the trees at the back of the house if the weather was nice, and on certain occasions, they were even allowed to go for a stroll downtown, to visit the shops where Gina was buying, little by little, the things necessary for her trousseau. Bianco paid the bills with discretion and pleasure. On none of these occasions did he manage to touch lightly so much as her hand, although more than once on Bianco's lips the conversation, having to do with the most diverse subjects, became passionately enthused and Gina appeared to listen to him with extraordinary attention. Bianco had, obviously, every so often, the desire to touch her, to possess her, especially in view of the fact that as Gina approached her majority, her body matured, bloomed, became firmer, fuller, more luxuriant, but he always abstained from doing so, although he never ceased to have the impression, worrisome and a little terrifying, that Gina would accept his advances, and would even yield to them, with the same passivity with which she had accepted all the rest. That passivity was, however, the opposite of obedience – as though Gina too had had her plans, vaster, more fathomless, more inevitable than Bianco's, and in the scheme of which Bianco would have been no more than a secondary, insignificant, interchangeable element.

Finally the wedding day arrived, when the house had already

been finished for several months. As the ceremony took place *en famille*, Garay López did not come from Buenos Aires, but he urged Bianco to come to the capital for his honeymoon. This seemed like a good idea to Bianco: immune to the charms of exogamy, which acquaints both the husband and the wife with an unknown part of the world and makes it familiar to both, annexing heterogeneous foreign areas, Bianco preferred to emphasize by his honeymoon in the capital the difference he intended to establish from then on with his in-laws, pointing out from the first the respective limits of each territory. But as the steamboat went downriver to the capital only on Sunday afternoons and they were married on a Saturday, they spent the first night at home.

They had left them alone. Since it was the end of October, it was turning hot, and though it was eleven at night, one could walk about comfortably in shirt sleeves through the rooms of the house and even the patios. They had brought them to the house in a carriage – the family had insisted that, in accordance with tradition, the banquet should be held in the house of the bridesmaid's parents – and when the horses went off down the dirt street, until the sound of their hoofs, as though a luminous substance formed part of its composition, faded away in the darkness, Bianco and Gina strolled for a time in the patios and then went into the bedroom. They had never spoken, not even by means of remote allusions, of what was about to happen, and Bianco, out of discretion, even though he felt his usual palpitations in the back of his neck and between his shoulder blades, preferred to go out for a moment into the patio to smoke a cigar while Gina changed. Every once in a while, he cast a quick glance toward the thin crocheted curtains that let the light inside pass through, and when he thought that Gina must be ready he slowly made his way to the bedroom door and after trying for several seconds to hear some sound coming from inside, he knocked twice with the knuckle of his index finger on the glass pane of the door.

"Yes," Gina's voice said, without any particular inflection.

Bianco pushed the door open and suddenly stopped in his tracks in the entryway: in the months that had elapsed, when they went downtown to make purchases to complete Gina's trousseau, even though Bianco, discreetly, confined himself to waiting outside as Gina, either alone or with her mother, chose the necessary lingerie, silky and diaphanous, intended to envelop and to hide her warm and distant flesh, and only entered the shops in order to pay the bill once the women had had the packages wrapped, and although he had at no time seen the objects for which he paid so willingly, not a night had gone by without his imagining Gina, covered by those smooth and transparent fabrics; hence when he saw that, lying in bed, after having removed the coverlet, Gina was stark naked on top of the white sheet, Bianco opened his eyes and his mouth inordinately wide, and arching his brick-colored eyebrows, turned two steps aside and leaned against the washbasin. Doubtless Gina's body, matte, full of firm and well-proportioned curves, with that surprising strip of dark down that descended from her navel to the black triangle of her pubis forming a peremptory arrow that pointed to the rough protuberance that afforded a glimpse of its reddish reverse side, and doubtless her eyes too, open and calm, that looked at him with their usual frankness, without modesty or obscenity, were the cause of Bianco's pounding heart and his confusion, but it was above all the expression of her oval face that perturbed him, the direct, literal manner in which that expression appeared to show that Gina had deciphered the euphemisms, circumlocutions, allusions of those two years of waiting, from the moment that he had first laid eyes on the whirling hem of her dress above her little white shoes up to the very last few seconds when he had knocked on the glass pane of the door of the bedroom with the knuckle of his index finger. Deep within himself, but with fleeting pains like whiplashes that at times abruptly reached the surface, Bianco felt that there was something unknown, inaccessible in Gina, an unexpected element that escaped his grasp, a proportion of indefinable force that he must henceforth take into account in all his calculations and that he could control only blindly, knowing that, if freed, that force was capable of bringing on unpredictable and destructive reactions.

Since he had had one of his family's day laborers build the cabin for Bianco, Garay López had not returned to the city; but Bianco traveled to Buenos Aires every summer, prolonging, in his long conversations in several languages, the copious, ironic correspondence, full of allusions and differences of opinion, that they sent each other regularly. Bianco's marriage aroused a vague and ethereal skepticism in Garay López: according to him, the thinker and the artist are not meant to create a family; artists and thinkers are already a family among themselves, they mutually fecundate each other, and engender, to employ his own words, that impalpable and imperishable progeny, the works of the spirit. But not only did Garay López put his own house at their disposal for the duration of the honeymoon trip, moving to a hotel, but was waiting for them at the door, looking more elegant than ever, having carefully calculated in front of the mirror the discreet harmony of the dull colors of his attire. Bianco got off the boat first, so as not to keep him waiting, as Gina finished getting ready, and after a moment of jovial conversation, they saw her appear on the gangplank. Two red spots suddenly showed up on Garay López's pale cheeks.

"Congratulations, cher ami," he murmured gravely, without even turning his head toward Bianco, on seeing Gina's tall body, svelte and undulating, her firm legs outlined against her yellow dress with every step, as she came down the gentle slope of the gangplank until the soles of her shoes touched the pier.

"I entrust you to the only friend I have left in all of South America," Garay López said, after having kissed Gina's hand at length, and it seemed to Bianco that he perceived, in the somewhat distracted irony with which he uttered the words, a confused emotion, a sort of agitation, as though he had lacked air at the moment of pronouncing them. Garay López's habit of squeezing the hand of the person to whom he was talking and keeping it captive during the first sentences of the conversation, which had always caused Bianco a certain annoyance when it was a question of his own hand, made him a little impatient instead, now that the hand was Gina's, and her expression of delighted astonishment at Garay López's effusions would have seemed shocking to him if, in a moment of distraction on the part of Garay López, Gina had not cast a quick, furtive, vaguely pleading glance at him, as though she were begging him to rescue her from the situation.

They went to stay at Garay López's house, and during the first three days, after he had shown them through all the rooms and given instructions to the maid and the cook, Garay López did not appear again. As Gina was getting dressed to go out, Bianco examined Garay López's library, with skepticism. Although he had been in it several times before, he had never had the opportunity to look through it at his leisure, and he was not astonished at not being astonished to discover in it many of the authors who were the principal gods of the positivist religion: he had already observed that Garay López concealed many of his real convictions in order to be gracious to him, an attitude that Bianco appreciated, but that in his heart of hearts he regarded as being unnecessary, since, because he considered Garay López as being immature and rather eccentric, more of an artist than a thinker, he did not attribute to him any great philosophical stature, and tolerated his convictions with condescension. On the third day, Garay López came to call on them, proving by his every action, in a rather ostentatious way – which must have seemed to him the height of discretion – that as long as they were there, he would regard himself as paying a visit to someone else's house.

"But this is your house," Gina said, laughing, as Garay López, with his eyes half-closed, kept shaking his head, repeating "No, no, no, no, no," in a serious, determined way, so as to prove that such a conception of things was inadmissible. When she was alone with Bianco, Gina imitated him, making mock of him. But when he came to visit them or take them on an outing, they spent the time laughing and talking together. Remaining a little off to one side, Bianco watched them: except for Garay López's paleness – one would have said that he did everything possible so as not to get a tan in summer – which contrasted with Gina's matte complexion, they resembled each other so closely physically that they could pass for brother and sister: they were of exactly the same height, and when the three of them strolled about together, with Bianco always in the middle, his brick-colored hair barely reached the chins of Gina and of Garay López, who frequently addressed each other above his head. Garay López's hair and well-trimmed beard were as sleek as Gina's hair and had the same coal-black color; apart from the shade of their skin, their hands, long, delicate and bony, were identical; and he could have said the same about their eyes, which both of them were in the habit of opening wide and riveting on him, an insistent and frank look, of a transparency disturbed only by dark flashes, at times lighting up with a supplementary gleam, which in Garay López came from insolence and in Gina from some unfathomable sentiment of which perhaps not even she herself was conscious. And although Gina, almost the moment Garay López had left them, heaved exaggerated sighs, to show that Garay López's presence exhausted her, the following day Bianco could see that the jovial interchanges began once again, causing a very slight, almost unacknowledged anxiety in him, and a more and more conscious desire, if a complicity really existed, hidden perhaps even from themselves, to oblige them to reveal it. More than peace of mind, what he was confusedly seeking was certainty, although, to tell the truth, he didn't know what sort of certainty it was, of some new truth about things, of some point of view that, during the forty-five years that he had been alive, had not formed part of his preoccupations, or if it had, it was necessary to go back to the obscure years, that period in his life, before he reached the age of thirty, which, by dint of wanting it to be vague for everyone else, had ended up being so for himself as well. Bianco felt that if that complicity existed, and he was the only one aware of its existence, the situation was still more humiliating for him, as though it had been brought about not by Gina and Garay López, but by the evil energy of the secondary embodied in them, avid ramifications foreign both to the good and to the evil of a series of coincidences between substance and temperature which exhausts itself simply in the momentum of their transformations.

"Tomorrow is my day off at the hospital, and I want you to lend me Gina, cher ami, to help me buy some presents for my sisters, providing, of course, that Gina is willing," Garay López said one night when the three of them were dining together at the restaurant of his hotel.

"In fact, it's the ideal day, because I have a number of business matters not yet settled that I must attend to, and I was troubled by the thought of leaving Gina alone all day long," Bianco replied, after remaining lost in thought for a few seconds as happened every time that he gave an affirmative answer to a proposal that fitted in perfectly with his own plans.

"I promise to bring her back to you by nightfall," Garay

López answered.

On the following morning, around ten, Garay López came by to get her and, when they had left, Bianco, instead of getting dressed and going out as he had intended, went back to bed, and for a couple of hours lay there waiting for the two of them to return. All during that time, he kept telling himself: "In any case they won't be back before nightfall; it's not worth it to wait for them," but every so often he seemed to hear the sound of the outside door, Gina's voice, Garay López's laughter, familiar steps resounding in the rooms and approaching the bedroom. Two or three times, making a superhuman effort, he went to the window overlooking the street to see if they were coming. At around one o'clock in the afternoon, without at any time thinking of how strange his conduct was, he got dressed and went to see the two or three businessmen with whom he had business to transact. But he scarcely even listened to what the others told him and his famous pragmatic sense, which he pretended not to take seriously, and which at times he talked about as other people speak of the ease with which they spit between their teeth, seemed to have ceased functioning since morning. He ended his business calls as soon as possible and went out into the street. Two or three times along every block, it seemed to him that he saw Gina and Garay López, going in or out of a shop, a house, riding in a hired carriage, and Gina's yellow dress, the same one she was wearing when she came down the gangplank, that to his startled surprise she had put on that morning, appeared to be omnipresent, floating and vanishing, here and there, in the streets of Buenos Aires. Finally, around four, he went back to the house, and sitting down in an armchair opposite the front door, began waiting for them to return. Second after second, minute after minute, hour after hour, all he did was wait: he was paralyzed for any other sort of action, for action in general, and the odd thing was that he did not think about anything else, he did not imagine or suspect anything, he did not attribute to Gina and to Garay López any particular intention; he was merely anxious to know whether that blind hostile force, whose presence he thought he had perceived in Garay López and in Gina, had also revealed itself to them and he was impatient to recognize in their faces the proof of that revelation. The room gradually grew darker as he waited, motionless, proceeding from one instant to the next just as, in a dream, one proceeds from one step to the next of a staircase that leads to empty space, until, closer to eight o'clock than to seven, he heard the sound of the front door opening, and leaping up from the armchair, ran to the bedroom and flung himself on the bed, so that when Gina came into the bedroom she had to shake him gently several times, because he was pretending to be sleeping soundly. Gina brushed his cheek with her lips and Bianco noted that she seemed annoyed. He washed his face and tidied himself up a bit, exactly as if he had been sleeping for hours on end, and with a jovial, nonchalant air, entered the living room, where Gina had turned on the lights.

"I think I slept too long," he said.

"We've prepared a surprise for you that will wake you up," Garay López said.

The brick-colored eyebrows arched slightly.

"Gina, you have to be the one," Garay López said.

"No," Gina said gravely. "You're the one whose idea it was."

Bianco noticed Gina's increasing annoyance, and waited for a few seconds. Finally Garay López, from among the numerous packages piled up on the table, removed one which barely fit in the palm of his hand, wrapped in rough paper, that appeared to have absorbed some sort of grease, and held it out to Bianco:

"It's to stimulate your imagination," Garay López said.

Bianco took the package and unwrapped it: it was a metal object, no larger than the palm of his hand, a metal bar some six inches long and two inches wide, the ends of which were curved upward, forming a sort of U with a straight back, a little wider than the two vertical sides, on each one of which was a hole. The two holes were at the same level, and putting the object in front of his right eye, Bianco looked at Garay López through the holes.

"A turnbuckle for tightening fence wire," he said.

"That's why we wanted to go by ourselves, to give you a surprise, cher ami," Garay López said, with a smile that Bianco could see through the aligned holes of the turnbuckle.

Although Garay López's plural struck him as slightly improper, and in a certain sense paradoxical, since instead of including Gina it served rather to define a whimsical projection of Garay López's with regard to the situation, Bianco ignored it, and hefting the turnbuckle with discreet enthusiasm, looked questioningly at Garay López:

"A German friend," Garay López said with satisfaction, "can put us in touch with the manufacturer."

Bianco nodded his head slowly and repeatedly, already thinking of the practical consequence of the matter: for several years now, he had been planning to promote wire fencing on the pampas in order to enclose fields, whose boundaries were vague, and in the face of the resistance of traditional landowners to adopt the system, it had occurred to him that, if he made Garay López his partner, he would be introducing a Trojan horse among the cattle ranchers of the province – including Garay López's brother, despite the hatred that existed between them, or perhaps precisely because of that hatred, he could not be opposed to the plan – and since Bianco was convinced of the advantages of the system, he was of the opinion that, if a few accepted it, sooner or later all the rest would end up adopting it. Garay López had hesitated for a long time before accepting his proposal, and the nods of Bianco's head, accompanied by a pensive smile that, for some strange reason, attenuated for a moment the bitter set of his lips, were the result of the unexpected satisfaction that Garay López's present brought him, the present with which he gave him, in coded form and a bit melodramatically, as was his habit, his reply. Garay López looked at him with his usual irony, but in his gaze now there were waves of emotion of which his own acts were the cause, since his slightly ostentatious emotion, or emotion ostentatiously repressed, seemed to come over him from his supposing a certain hidden emotion on Bianco's part because of his having received the gift. But if there was any emotion on Bianco's part, it was occasioned less by that bar of iron curved in the form of a U, with two holes lined up on the vertical sides, than because he was thinking: "Before this trip, when I talked to him about my plan to put wire fencing around the fields, his reaction was sarcastic, if not contemptuous, although he pretended to be interested in it, and now, as if by chance, just when I've married, he gets ahead of me in everything and is already acting as though he were my partner."

"Gina, thank you. Thank you, caro dottore," Bianco said, and though Garay López smiled in satisfaction at his words, Gina's displeasure, instead of lessening, appeared to grow as she listened to them. Gina picked up several packages from the table, and disappeared in the direction of the bedroom. And when Garay López finally left, refusing an invitation to dinner because he was on duty at the hospital that night, Bianco went into the bedroom and found Gina stretched out on the bed in the darkness, and although she was lying motionless, Bianco realized that she wasn't asleep. He was eager to scrutinize her face, examine it carefully, weigh each one of her gestures to see if the adverse power, which he was convinced had entered her, had already made its presence evident to her. To his surprise, Gina spoke to him in the darkness, in a voice broken with sobs:

"You've made me waste the whole day looking for that piece of iron. This is the last time I'm coming to Buenos Aires. I thought it was our honeymoon," Gina's voice said in the darkness, between sobs. "And your Antonio, your Antonio! What a bore! I'm not married to him. I don't have any reason to go with him to buy presents for his sisters, and take them to them."

Lying down beside her in the darkness, Bianco prepared to console her, surprised to hear Gina cry for the first time since he had known her; and the reasons were so unexpected and so trivial that Bianco smiled briefly in the darkness; in a certain sense, Gina's very existence terrified him, and the fact that that existence would be spent from now on in proximity to his own seemed to him to be an inconceivable, dangerous situation, although, to tell the truth, he, who contemplated every situation from a sort of frigid, disinterested height, had only a vague presentiment of danger and terror, which, instead of bringing them to the surface of his awareness, caused him to grow rigid, to assume an attitude of extreme, permanent vigilance, like someone who, walking about in the darkness, knows that he may receive a blow but is unable to anticipate from what point in the blackness it will come. Just as a magnet attracts iron filings, Gina attracted all his thoughts, but also like the iron filings, moving about more and more swiftly and inexorably through the magnetic field, his thoughts knew nothing about the force that was attracting them. And stroking Gina's hair, brushing with his white fingers her cheeks down which he felt the tears streaming, he began to talk to her about Garay López, telling her that even though he was immature, she must not forget that he was his only friend and his partner as well, who had lent them his house to spend their honeymoon in, and that at this very moment they were in fact lying in his bed. Ceasing little by little to weep, Gina seemed to listen to him with that excessive attention, and excessive credulity as well, accepting what he said

in its most literal meaning, instead of for what he might be
silently implying, hinting at or suggesting, that attention that
was less obedience than naïveté, and so singleminded that in the
midst of his efforts to calm her and induce her to accept Garay
López, Bianco wondered at one point if he were not going too
far, and even if he ought not admit to Gina certain evident
defects in Garay López, his insolence for example. But he
couldn't do it: without his realizing it, Gina's criticisms of Garay
López, after his long wait that day, had caused him to experience
a certain disillusionment.

"In any case, don't make me spend another entire day being
bored by him," Gina said to him, laughing, and embracing him
in the darkness.

But the following night, when Garay López came to eat with
them, Gina gave proof of the same voluble affection for him as
on the days before, and when, on his arrival, Garay López kissed
her hand and held it between his own for a good while, as he
uttered a few witty phrases, Gina did not cast toward him,
Bianco, any furtive, pleading look. They seemed made of the
same substance, the same springy dough, juvenile and excitable,
that has been kneaded down only once and then divided into
two equal halves so as to give them form and send them out
into the world, forever bearing the mark of a common origin,
and even their difference of sex appeared to be blurred, for if the
abundance of gestures, the high-pitched, affected tones of voice
and the sighs of Garay López had something feminine about
them, Gina's stature, her rather bony hands, were like the mascu-
line residues of her person, and, as though a combination of
these androgynous excesses in a common space, they appeared
to balance and complement each other. The confidence that
reigned between them was so great that Bianco, discreetly
observing them, was a little sorry to have been so forbearing
with regard to Garay López the night before, in the bedroom,

and, being careful above all that none of these troubled thoughts would come out into the open to betray him, readied himself to confront, in the future, that force that challenged him.

Seated in the wicker armchair by the bedroom door, Bianco contemplates the sunny patio, where the warmth of the light, of the peaceable air of October, which do not contrive to contaminate his dizzying, somber thoughts, reach even the porch. Gina's nearness, as she lies stretched out on the bed in the semidarkness, reaches him as though in strong gusts from the bedroom. In order to forget about her, Bianco gets to his feet and heads for his study, crossing the sunny patio, passing beneath the overhanging roof of the porch opposite, and making a brief detour through the living room to get the bottle of cognac and a glass that he takes with him to the study, setting them down on the desk. Bianco sits down, pours himself a little cognac, drinks it down, and again pouring himself a little more sets the bottle back on the desk. The cognac trickles slowly down his throat, down his esophagus, and Bianco feels its slightly burning passage until it spreads through his stomach, and almost immediately beads of sweat begin to run down his back, as at the same time the alcohol, filtering through the secret folds of his body, makes his thoughts seem more remote, padded by a sort of warm fog, more painless and impersonal, as though they were someone else's. In his mouth, on his tongue, just a few seconds after having swallowed it, he begins to perceive the taste of it, as a pleasant supplementary accompaniment which in all truth he has not been seeking, and of which he is not even aware, perhaps because the real relief that he was looking for in the swallow of cognac consisted of it muffling his thoughts, giving them an orderly rhythm, reigning over them, and having succeeded in doing so, his capacity for satisfaction is momentarily saturated and does not seek to spread out into other agreeable sensations. And when he takes the second glass, the brick-colored crop of curls hanging down at each side of his forehead begin to grow damp, cling together, and stick to his temples. On the desk, his papers lie undisturbed, neatly arranged in two piles that leave the center of the desk clear, except for the elongated silver inkwell, with two receptacles for the ink and a groove in which several penholders are lying. The two piles of papers and notebooks, at either side of the desk, have been personally arranged by Bianco, according to a simple principle yet one that Bianco regards at the same time as rational and symbolical: on the right, the business letters, the account books, the papers having to do with the countryside, his cattle, his various landholdings, his commercial projects; on the left, his philosophical notes to be used to prepare his refutation of the positivists, quotations copied from certain treatises, reflections written at night, after dinner, résumés of his meditations at the cabin, and even old letters from Garay López containing a number of observations by his partner concerning these problems. To Bianco, without the slightest doubt the left part of his body harbors all his spiritual and philosophical components, whereas the right half is the seat of his pragmatic elements.

Bianco pours himself a third cognac, knowing beforehand that if the first served to lessen the velocity of his thoughts and render them distant and painless, and the second to separate him from the world, placing it in a closed system in which he sees those painless thoughts floating, as in a test tube in which a vacuum has previously been created, so as to enable him to examine them one by one, dissecting and classifying them, the third, now almost unnecessary, has no other function than to allow him to perform certain outward movements as he focuses his attention on what is happening inside him. But he has not yet finished pouring it and immobilizing himself in his chair, when a pair of discreet knocks make him raise his head in the direction of the door that opens out onto the porch.

"May I come in?" Gina's voice says from outside, and before Bianco has time to answer her, she pushes the door open and peeks into the study.

"Of course," Bianco says.

When Gina begins to walk over toward the desk, Bianco notes that she is barefoot and that, with each step, her feet, rising slightly, reveal a sole black with dust.

"Were you working?" Gina asks.

"No, no," Bianco says. "I was drinking a cognac, and wanted to put some papers in order."

Gina draws a chair up and sits down across from him, on the other side of the desk. For a few seconds, she looks at him thoughtfully, and then says to him gravely, though she is already thinking about something else:

"Don't drink so much."

"That's the third one I've had, and only half a glass each time," Bianco says.

"I don't know how anyone can drink cognac in this heat," Gina says.

"It isn't all that hot," Bianco says.

Gina doesn't answer him. She lowers her gaze, reflects for a few seconds, and then once again raises toward Bianco her big eyes, wide open, at once unfathomable and frank, a brilliant double wall behind which there teem dark masses of secret life that Bianco manages neither to recognize nor to intuit.

"My period is three weeks late," Gina says. "I think I'm pregnant."

Suddenly, all of Bianco's pores seem to open at once, and as though he had put on a shirt soaking wet with perspiration, he feels the sweat running down his back, his chest, his arms, and at the same time he begins to perceive rhythmical palpitations at the back of his neck and between his shoulder blades.

"Three weeks?" he says, trying to keep his voice from

trembling and succeeding only with great difficulty.

"Yes, three weeks," Gina says. "I didn't tell you before, because I wanted to be sure."

"Sure of what?" Bianco says.

"Sure that my period wasn't going to come," Gina says.

Bianco nods his head, his face a little whiter than usual, his brick-colored hair stuck not only to his temples now but also to the round protuberances of his skull, and at the same time, stretching out his hand, he raises the glass of cognac and takes a swallow, and then another, looking at the empty bottom of the glass for a few seconds before putting it back down on the desk.

"That's why I can't concentrate. It's not your fault if our experiment fails," Gina says.

"That has nothing to do with it," Bianco says. "Don't worry about it."

"It was that morning after you came back from the country. The day that Antonio came. I'm sure of it," Gina says.

Bianco pretends to be searching his memory.

"Yes, yes, I seem to remember now," he says.

"We've never talked about having children," Gina says. "I'm happy. But..."

"But what?" Bianco asks, with a quick smile that causes his white, almost blue lips to turn even paler, and deepens the very fine wrinkles around his eyes. "It's an excellent piece of news."

"We've never talked about having children," Gina says. "I thought you'd like to have several."

"Several?" Bianco says. "For the moment let's see how the first one turns out."

Gina bursts out laughing.

"You're right," she says. Her eyes stare into Bianco's again. "I don't want to interrupt you any longer," she murmurs to him, lowering her voice in an odd way.

Bianco withstands her gaze.

"It was to tell me something important," he murmurs in turn.

They go on looking at each other. The silence of the house, on a Sunday, in October, is suddenly so noticeable that it becomes solemn and omnipresent, traversed by that gaze that, although it too is silent, is full of murmurs, of flashes of thought, of experiences, of memories stuck to the reverse side of their pupils, of their foreheads, that flit about like butterflies, errant and phosphorescent, on the black stage set of each one of them, which, although close together in space, are infinitely distant, inaccessible to the other. "It's his," Bianco thinks, and then tells himself that if he asked her, she might answer by telling the truth, with the same fathomless simplicity with which she is now looking him in the eyes without blinking but that, in any case, whatever the answer, true or false, negative or affirmative, he will continue to be unable to verify it, that that series of events which took place that day at the end of August when, arriving from the cabin, he found her puffing on a cigar with an expression of intense pleasure in the company of Garay López, was already circulating through inaccessible passageways of organs and memory, has already turned into blood and tissues, an untransferable and incommunicable experience, farther from his grasp than the outer limits of the universe. Whether she admits it or denies it, Bianco thinks, at any event it is still the same deadly force, the same excremental and swampy magma in which, whether they realize it or not, they are wallowing and splashing. And, he thinks, when all is said and done, it would be best if it were his, so that they would at least know in what abominable substance they are imprisoned.

"We should go take a stroll down by the river," Bianco says. "In your condition, it is highly recommended."

"I'll get dressed," Gina says. But before leaving, she comes over to Bianco and brushes his cheek with her lips.

And, in the months that follow, Gina's belly begins to grow. Bianco observes it from a distance, with frigid perplexity, like someone who studies, without any particular interest, the growth of a frog or the development of a plant, seeing how the features of Gina's face, her arms, her neck, her entire body, little by little grow more placid and heavy as her lower belly swells. During the summer months, fever, stampeding thoughts again take possession of Bianco. It is true that the heat is unbearable, full of shrill sounds, of murmurs, of blind insects and mosquitoes which, mounting from the swamps, darken the air, as big and black as flies, driving both men and animals mad, and Bianco, in the sultry afternoons as storms threaten, sometimes remembers Garay López's terror of summer in the city. Moreover, in his innermost depths, Bianco has already formed an opinion about Gina, and often he imagines her, not only in the company of Garay López, but in that of all the men in the immediate vicinity; he is convinced that she is not only victim of that matter beyond measure that he detests, but that she also secretes it, and that, like those female insects which eroticize the branch of the tree they land on, Gina contaminates whatever she touches, and leaves a voluptuous trail wherever she passes. In the beginning, he is able to follow the evolution of his thoughts as far as what he regards as the very edge of delirium, but as that edge retreats farther and farther into the distance as the summer goes by, in those moments in which he tells himself: "This is no longer either pragmatic thought or pure thought but delirium," he does not know that what he began to call thought the month before he had already classified as delirium two months earlier, and he, Bianco, who has told Garay López so many times that the wise man is indifferent to heat or cold, to shelter or exposure to the elements, to gain or loss, often catches himself trembling when he sees how the leaves dry up in the February sun or the animals wander, in a daze, about the corrals. It is something nameless, it would never have entered my mind to be afraid that that would happen to me because it has no name, it is only names that terrify us, he sometimes thinks, diluting his cognac with cool water so as to be able to tolerate it on summer nights.

"Don't drink so much," Gina keeps saying to him gently, and Bianco stares at her, as though lost in thought, without blinking, for several moments, and then he shakes his head and gives a brief, brittle laugh:

"I'm the one who should be taking care of you in these months and not the other way around," he says to her softly. "Right now, for instance, you should be in bed."

And taking her by the arm, he slowly leads her to the bedroom, hurrying ahead a little when they are almost there so as to open the door for her, helping her to get undressed and into bed, entering on tiptoe later on, when she is already asleep and he is slightly tipsy, so as not to awaken her or startle her.

Autumn finally arrives. But after a storm with no rain, consisting exclusively of black clouds, of thunder and lightning, of wind and dust devils but not a single drop of water, not one, at the end of March the weather turns a little cooler for a week and then, immediately thereafter, in two or three days' time, the heat sets in again, stuffy and damp, against nature, making the air so sultry that even the mosquitoes, that fly up by the millions from the swamps, flutter about sluggishly. She is now eight months along; she is going to give birth soon, Bianco thinks. He has turned over in his mind for such a long time the possibility that someone else has fathered the baby, he has advanced so far along the black passageway he had entered unthinkingly that he is beginning to realize that, for him, it is preferable that it be someone else's child, that, instead of going back the way he has come along the dark passageway, he must go on, he must hope, wager, prove to himself that it belongs to another, the other, Garay López, that the child is one day older than Gina has told him that it is, but that Gina, he is certain, would not be willing to admit it even under torture. No, he thinks: Garay López is the one who is going to tell me so.

"I'm going to write him that Gina is eight and a half months pregnant, and about to give birth. The only thing he need do is make his calculations. If he was on top of her that afternoon, on top of her as she was lying face up with the cushion under her buttocks, in the middle of the bed, he'll soon be turning up here in the city."

Around 1854, some twenty leagues south of the city, not far from the Carcarañá River, he found out that there was a man living on the pampas with his family, in a miserable cabin, near the only tree for many leagues around. The man was around forty-five years old at that time, and he had traveled a little, having even gotten as far as the gates of Buenos Aires, because two or three years before, he had been a soldier in the Grand Army and then a deserter, and even after deserting he had gone on wandering about the pampas for several months, roaming as far as the borders of Indian territory, before going back to his province. Since he was a deserter, he stopped by his hut only very occasionally; he spent most of his time in the open country-side, sleeping out of doors in every sort of weather with the saddle of his horse for a pillow, slaughtering other people's cattle for food or dropping in at general stores to buy maté, tobacco and sugar, get drunk and disappear. He was a tall, silent, muscular halfbreed, who despite his vagabond life, paid a great deal of attention to his personal appearance, almost to the point of affectation, and among the knick-knacks that he carried about with him he always had a brush, a little mirror and a pair of scissors; the moment he reached the banks of the Carcarañá he took a dip, and had anybody passed by the desolate spots that he frequented and knew like the palm of his hand, it would not have been a rare sight to see him, without even having bothered to climb off his horse that was quietly grazing after he had deposited his sombrero between its ears, cutting his hair and his curly beard, using, carefully and slowly, the scissors with one hand and holding with the other the little mirror in which he meticulously observed, after each snip of his scissors, the result of his work. Even though he was rumored to have committed several murders and despite the fact that he wasn't very talkative, he was well received, because once he'd gotten fired up with his first gins he felt like singing, accompanying himself discreetly and not at all awkwardly on the guitar, and when he'd finished, he would look about for a moment without saying anything to his listeners and then give a timid, satisfied little laugh, still without having said a word, and hand the guitar back to the storekeeper. Then he would sit quietly in his corner and go on drinking till he turned rigid and a sort of grayish color, and picking up what he called his vices, that is to say, his maté, his tobacco, his sugar, which the storekeeper placed in a little sack for him, he would head straight for the patio, standing stiffly erect, mount his horse after a number of fruitless, dignified attempts, and disappear on the pampas.

The man had five children: the oldest, a boy of seventeen, two girls, fifteen and sixteen, a little girl of nine, and the littlest one, who looked like a Guaraní halfbreed, whom he had insisted on naming Waldo, the name of a colonel in the Grand Army under whom he had served and of whom he had fond memories even though the colonel had sent him to the stocks and to jail more than once. The little halfbreed Waldo, who was only a year old, was a dark-skinned, chubby baby, who, getting lost among the dogs and going about on all fours like them, spent his time sucking up his snot, with the result that when he grew up he still had the habit of twisting the corners of his lips slightly upward and making a sucking sound with the saliva between his teeth, as though he were really clearing his nose. The mother of this dark-skinned band in rags and tatters, whom the man kept getting pregnant on nights when he was drinking, whose face had marked Indian features, was still not even thirty-five, but she looked sixty, perhaps because of her weatherbeaten skin and the few dark brown decayed teeth she still had left in her mouth. The children were all surly and taciturn and they all hated the man intensely, with no ifs, ands or buts, as one, so that when they saw him appear in the distance on the pampas, sitting tall in the saddle, for one of those capricious and fleeting visits that generally took place as it was getting dark, they all muttered to themselves the same powerless, sullen curses.

They had their reasons. Ever since he had deserted the Army, ever since he had gone wandering about the vague frontier marking off Indian territory, the man, already distant and cruel to his family by inclination though presentable and even refined when dealing with strangers, had acquired the bad habit, when he was drunk, of raping his oldest daughters who, although they accepted their father's abuse with resignation, and even with slightly comical astonishment in the beginning because it was something so unexpected, they none the less never stopped wishing that the tyrant who took them into the open country-side at dawn to have his way with them would kick the bucket as soon as possible. Since they all slept one on top of the other in the cabin, even though the man tried to do what he did in secret, the rest of the family, except for Waldo, who still slept backside to backside next to the littlest girl, watched his nocturnal maneuvers closely while pretending to be asleep, when the man came in the dark to shake awake one of the older daughters and took her out into the countryside. It was hard to know how he had decided to go into action, how, amid the abject, irrepressible and obscure tuggings of his own being that unexpectedly kindled his desire, had transformed that desire into action, an event, an ineffaceable knot in the translucent flow of time, in his senses and in others', and a black spot in his memory. Perhaps without his realizing it, his travels had shown him the ridiculous, relative nature of that filthy, rickety ruin in which they lived, in the shade of the only tree visible for many leagues around, the contingent essence of his own family, a bunch of obscure and anemic larvae crawling about on the empty pampas, beneath an empty sky, the absurdity of his own life as a deserter, as an incomprehensible, naked animal, the insistent strangeness that makes conventions unreal and makes of everything that lives and palpitates beneath the implacable sun a bland, undifferentiated and transitory magma. The fact remained that, on the nights when he'd gone on a binge, when he didn't sleep in some remote spot on the pampas, he came to the cabin on horseback and allowed himself to be carried away by his desire till the first pale light of dawn, when he mounted his horse once again and was lost from sight on the horizon.

The older son was a day laborer in landholdings along the south shore of the river, and sometimes, when they had to transport cattle, he went with the cowhands and for weeks he was not to be seen around the cabin, but when he came back he never forgot to bring a bit of money and a few little presents for his mother and his sisters. He stayed for a few days, thinking about how he was going to go about getting his family out of that indescribable ruin of a cabin, with its twisted uprights, its beams from which there hung bits of half-rotten straw, out of that sort of vacant lot covered with dung and dog shit, with unlikely, useless, broken objects that they had been collecting like rodents around their burrows, out of that bit of pampas that they had worn down to bare earth in their aimless goings and comings around the dwelling and where it seemed as though, by a sort of cosmic discouragement, of melancholy, not a single blade of grass would ever grow again. On his return from one of his journeys, the sisters took him aside, where their mother wouldn't hear them, and told him that the man had come one night and that this time, instead of abusing them, as was his habit, he had taken the littlest girl out into the countryside. The son didn't say anything, but he half-closed his eyes, took a long puff on his cigarette, and slowly nodded his head, several times, as though what they had just told him confirmed the rightness of a decision that he had already made a long time before. A few feet away the little girl, like a more or less emaciated tiny bird, was flitting about in a circle so as to entertain Waldo, who was slowly crawling on all fours among the dogs.

Two or three days later, the man turned up at the cabin, at nightfall, as was his habit. His older son and the two older girls exchanged a quick glance, imperceptible in the semidarkness, dimly lighted by a little candle flame, and went off to go to sleep. As if he had had a presentiment of something, or perhaps overcome by remorse, or by hesitation because of the little girl's frailness, her asexuality, her body that was more reminiscent of that of a toad than that of a desirable object, the man lay stretched out on the floor all night long, next to his wife, who appeared to be sleeping, telling himself that at dawn he would be off and never again set foot in the cabin, believing that all of them were asleep and that he alone was being kept awake by his confused desires, his terrors, his drowsing traversed by sudden starts and shudders. But when dawn came, and he got up to leave, going out into the reddish air of the pampas, something made him turn around, mechanically, from outside, with his feet practically in the stirrups already, and head for the corner of the cabin where the little girl slept. It was as if on going outdoors to the pampas and seeing the reddish patch coloring the sky in the east and making the outlines of the tree and the ranch gleam, he had said to himself that it wasn't worth the trouble, that on seeing the blinding sun appear in the empty sky once more in order to begin yet again its indifferent and monotonous passage, its obstinate and periodic course, it was preferable to retrace his steps, to yield to the undifferentiated, to melt once again into the anonymous night that awaited him in the cabin. Trying not to make any noise, he went over and shook the little girl quietly, almost tenderly, believing that in this way he would not awaken the others, and on seeing him at her side, in the first light of day that was already pouring in through the innumerable cracks everywhere in the cabin, the little girl opened her eyes, and without saying a word, sleepily rose to her feet to follow him, because after all it was only her father, and before going with him, more or less out of habit, she shook Waldo, as she did almost every morning when it began to get light, but her father shook his head, so the little girl followed him through the reddish semidarkness of the cabin, without noticing that Waldo was walking behind them, rubbing his eyes with the back of his hands. The three of them went out into the reddish air of dawn, which seemed to be crisscrossed with bloody filaments, and headed toward the tree, the father in front, the little girl behind him, almost touching him, walking in a cadence and a manner so much like her father's, the two of them thereby clearly showing a family resemblance, so that the little girl seemed to be parodying him, and the dark-skinned Waldo a few meters behind, tottering on his plump little legs, until, waking up all of a sudden because of the cool morning air, realizing that he would make better progress on all fours, he dropped to the ground and began crawling.

They were about to reach the tree, still at the same distance from each other, when the older son first, the girls a couple of seconds later, appeared at the door of the cabin, the son carrying a sharp-pointed shovel, the edge of which, on being struck by the first sunbeams, sparkled faintly in the early morning light, and the girls with two pieces of wood, two thin but heavy and compact tree trunks, of ñandubay perhaps, and began to head toward the first trio walking swiftly, at a resolute pace, so that they were fast lessening the distance that separated them. Finally, the mother appeared in the doorway, and leaning against the rough-hewn door frame with her hand gripping the burlap sack that served as a door, in such a way that at her back there could be seen the semidarkness inside because of the burlap sack's having been drawn aside, opened her mouth, revealing a black cavity that appeared to be a copy of the darkness against which her broad silhouette, looking somewhat tamped down, as though she had received a hammer blow on her head when she was a child, stood out clearly, thanks to the contrast with the reddish light that bled onto her body. From where she was standing, she watched the scene disinterestedly, almost indifferently: she saw the first group arrive alongside the tree and the second, brandishing the shovel and the tree trunks, gradually catching up with it.

"Not the little girl, no, you're not going to touch the little girl again!" the older son said as he caught up with his father, who at just that moment, and without having realized that even Waldo was following him on all fours, turned around to grab the little girl's arm and draw her to him. On catching sight of his son, the father instinctively raised his hand to his belt, in order to take out his knife, but the son leaped toward him with the sharp end of the shovel raised to hit him, so that the man, knowing that he would not have time, or perhaps because he did not want to unsheathe his weapon to use against his son, began to step back. They were near the enormous, bushy tree, whose trunk was so large, full of protruding, fibrous knots, that the day it became hollow, which was bound to happen sooner or later, all of them could have lived inside it or on top of it, as did other poor people on the pampas, a trunk that formed a sort of hard covering full of deep depressions at the foot of the tree, and then enormous roots that stood out from the ground like petrified tentacles, against one of which, as he stepped backwards, the man stumbled, and after vainly waving his arms in the air in an attempt to keep his balance, ended up sprawled out on the ground. "I've already told you no, not the little girl, that you're not going to touch the little girl again!" the son shouted to him once more, flinging himself on him and hitting him over the head with the shovel, again and again, with such fury and swiftness that one of the times when he raised the shovel he brushed the shoulder of the little girl, making her stagger and fall among the twisted tree roots. The man kicked and shouted, in tears, saying, "No, my son, no my son, no my son," not addressing anyone in particular, not even his son, and the proof that it was merely a pleading interjection, addressed, rather than to his son or to the world in general, to himself perhaps, since there seemed to be a note of desperate reproach in his voice as he uttered the words, was that when the son left the shovel suspended in midair for a moment and his big sisters took advantage of the moment to come over to the fallen man and hit him over the head with the tree trunks, the man kept on repeating, "No, my son, no my son, no my son," more and more feebly, his face and his head mangled by the blows, until the blood gushing out choked him and he lay there without moving.

Waldo the mestizo had not moved in the beginning either, when his older brother had gone over to the man and raised the shovel, holding it aloft all ready to strike. But when the man stepped backward, and tripping over the root, had sprawled out on the ground, Waldo let out a wail and began to cry, circling about on all fours and nervously sucking in his snot, as the older brother and the girls beat on the head the man stretched out against the tree roots, writhing and groaning with each blow. From where she was lying on the ground, the girl watched the scene with eyes opened wide, but more out of astonishment or curiosity than terror, and the woman, who had been gotten pregnant with this brood on nights of drunkenness, on seeing them create havoc from afar next to the tree and then the man lying motionless, disdainfully let the burlap sack fall back into place, and without making the slightest gesture or uttering a single word, disappeared inside the semidarkness of the cabin.

For half a minute at least, the man's older children stopped dealing him blows on the head and stood there in silence, so that, all across the pampas, nothing was heard except Waldo's wailing; he was now sitting on his buttocks amid little bits of dry sticks, dry brushwood, dry dog turds and horseshit, and without ceasing to howl was mechanically gathering together with his plump little hand fistfuls of sandy dirt and throwing them in the air, again and again, with nervous, rhythmical movements, as though he were trying to dispel his panic in the sandy dust whose lightest particles, which remained floating in the air, took on thickness and corporeality on being traversed by the first horizontal rays of the sun, which was now an intensely red semicircle stuck fast to the nearby horizon. The older son and the girls, without letting go of the shovel and the tree trunks, appeared to be hesitating distractedly, beginning perhaps to realize at that very moment what they had just done, without hearing Waldo's wailing or paying any attention to their little sister, who was still looking at them with her eyes very wide open, but when the man, who appeared to be dead, moved his battered head a little against the tree roots, the three of them threw themselves on him again, all at the same time, and began to beat him furiously until they realized that he wasn't going to move again. Then the older brother let go of the shovel, and noticing Waldo's weeping, bent down toward him to lift him up, but the youngster began to weep even harder when his brother's arms reached out toward him, and letting himself fall to one side, got down on all fours and began to make his escape as fast as he could go. When his older brother stopped chasing him, Waldo stopped, still wailing at the top of his lungs and sucking up his snot, but when his brother gave signs of coming closer to him, Waldo cried out even more loudly, and drew away as fast as he could crawl. Finally, his brother, taking pity on him, left him in peace, and turned toward his little sister, who let him pick her up in his arms but did not stop looking over her brother's shoulder at their father's head, lying pounded to pieces against the tree roots.

They left him stretched out on the ground and went to drink their morning maté on the other side of the cabin, so as not to have to see him all during the time they were having breakfast, and discussing what they would do with the body, since the women wanted to throw him into the Carcarañá and the son preferred to bury him on the pampas. The mother didn't say a word: she came and went with the maté gourd, without erasing from her face a sardonic smile, more visible in her eyes than on her mouth, puckered up from her lack of teeth. She paused at times to listen to the conversation, with the maté gourd held in both hands resting on her belly; realizing finally that that persistent little smile meant "Say whatever you like, but I saw how you killed him," the son impatiently grabbed the shovel and tying up the man's body with a rope that he passed underneath his arms, mounted his horse, dragging the body behind, and went off to bury him on the pampas, in fallow ground, little more than a league from the cabin. He looked for a place where the fallow fields would hide the earth that he had removed until the rain would erase all traces, and he dug deeply, for a couple of hours; before dumping the body into the hole he relieved it of the weight of the knife and the belt, in which the man had tucked a few pesos, and after crossing himself he began to cover the body with dirt. When he reached the top of the hole he devoted considerable time to leveling the terrain and covering it with grass so as to hide the grave. Without marking the spot with a cross or anything else, he picked up the shovel and rode off at a gallop. In the middle of the fallow ground, mute and covered over with earth, the man remained; the last traces of his passage across the pampas would little by little be effaced by the rain and the wind.

When the son returned to the cabin, he saw that the women, in a circle around the door, were all bent over looking at something that was lying on the ground, and on dismounting from his horse, he saw that it was Waldo, lying there curled up in a ball, with his face covered with his forearms, and on reaching his side he could hear that his howls, which could still be heard in the vicinity of the cabin as he was taking the corpse away to bury it, had been transformed into a low animal-like whine, broken but insistent, like the one that he had sometimes heard coming from dying puppies or baby pigeons that had fallen from their nest. At nightfall, Waldo finally fell silent, but during the night he went on whimpering in his sleep; in the days that followed, at any moment of the day or night, the feeble, abrupt moans began again, intermittent signs, so appropriate to the place that had witnessed their birth, like the cries of nameless beasts or the twinkling of ice-cold stars over that barren patch of earth, laid bare by the going and coming of their somber, forsaken bodies. After a few months they became accustomed to the moans as they had already done with regard to the rather anachronistic presence of the tree or the empty horizon.

The mother died during the year and after burying her the children went their own way. The son enlisted as a soldier, in Entre Ríos, and his sisters followed him, mingling with the noisy horde of virile, loudmouthed women camp followers who, of all the soldiers who copulated with them underneath a cart or in the high weeds, ended up attaching themselves to one of them until the Indians slit his throat or the very same officer for

whom he had made maté on nights when he was on guard duty
had him shot as a deserter. But before crossing the Paraná, heading north, they had left their little sister and Waldo in Coronda,
where there were some houses, a chapel, and six or seven nice
little garden plots that the droughts burned to a crisp or floods
wiped out. The village priest found them sleeping in the doorway of the chapel, kept them with him for a couple of months,
and then found them a place with a family of Asturians, with
the understanding that, in exchange for board and lodging, the
little girl would stay behind to do the housework and care for
the children when their parents went out to work in the fields.

Waldo no longer whined, either by day or by night, but neither did he utter a single word. Every so often, he would get
upset, tremors would come over him, and when he grew restless,
he would leap in the air, with his arms bent at the elbow, his
hands crossed at the level of his chest, accelerating the tic that
had remained with him from the time when he still went about
on all fours, namely sucking up his mucus by twisting the corners of his mouth upward and making his saliva hiss between his
teeth. At other times, he took to shaking his head endlessly, as
though he were making a sempiternal sign of assent – to the
impenetrable order of things, perhaps, of which he may have
managed to see, in a devastating lightning flash, some archaic
and abominable vestige. But he didn't say a word. When he
wanted something, a caramel, for example, because he was
extremely fond of sweets, he would begin to give little leaps or
nod his head faster, and the little girl, who in the beginning tried
to teach him to talk, immediately understood the cause of his
excitement, and gave him then and there the treat he wanted.

It is hard to understand how things become common knowledge on the pampas. For league after league there was scarcely a
handful of scattered dwellings, isolated from each other, lost,
not to say forgotten, on the expanse of flat land, suitable only

for Indians and cattle, where everything that is alive in the countryside is nearly a day's journey on horseback from the villages that are closest, and yet, in the hamlet of Coronda and in all the countryside around, the little girl, without her knowing it, went by the name of La Violadita – the Little Girl Who Had Been Raped – more in a compassionate voice than in a reproachful one. When she finally discovered, when she was thirteen or fourteen, that that was what people called her, she didn't even know what the word meant, but since the nickname seemed to make the parish priest feel sorry for her, she began calling herself that too, a little out of coquetry and above all, when she needed something, so as to awaken people's compassion and get it more easily. The truth is that when the Asturians, tired of starving in the countryside and of waiting for the lands that the government had promised them, of seeing Indians and soldiers pass their way who wantonly destroyed everything in their path, decided to seek their fortune in Rosario, Waldo and La Violadita settled in a cabin on the outskirts of the village, and La Violadita filled it with religious images and little statues of saints that the priest gave her when she went to tidy up for him in the sacristy.

They let them live in peace. La Violadita spent what she earned cleaning and taking care of children on sweets for Waldo and on candles to burn before the images that the village priest offered her: at any hour of the day, there were always a pair of candles lighted, which La Violadita stuck with melted wax to a little round piece of wood for a base, and which floated in a basin full of water so as not to set fire to the cabin. Short and tubby, with a big mouth like a toad's, which he never closed all the way and which revealed two rows of incredibly white and perfect teeth, despite the quantity of sweets he ate, Waldo followed her everywhere, taking short little steps that at times forced him to trot. At the age of nine, he had never said one word, until one day the miracle took place.

La Violadita had grown. At seventeen, her little frog's body had filled out quite a bit, and she had turned out to be as tall as her father, with huge almond eyes and brown skin, smooth and gleaming, which again like her father, she was in the habit of washing constantly. She liked to dress in white and also carefully, almost manicly, saw to it that her brother was neat and clean. She now had two pretty breasts, set far apart with pointed ends, like two pears, at which the older boys of the village cast furtive glances, knowing that the parish priest was watching over her and that, in spite of having been raped, and perhaps because of that very fact, La Violadita had no interest in those things that the boys would have been more than ready to teach her. But they were not too insistent, or didn't even dare to suggest it, and perhaps it even cooled their ardor in advance when they saw that La Violadita's consuming passions were getting candles for her saints and sweets for Waldo. Only one of them tried to go any farther, one moreover who wasn't all that young any more, a certain Costa, who acted as sheriff in the town and was in the habit of going to the cabins on the outskirts to propose to the young girls that they spend a little time with him in exchange for a present, a proposition that the girls often accepted, sometimes because they wanted to and at other times because they felt obliged to. Costa began to make advances to La Violadita, who seemed not only to fail to understand, but not even to listen to his hints and perhaps she really didn't listen to them or understand them, since beneath a tree on the pampas, eight or nine years before, in two or three dizzying couplings, she had experienced to the full what Costa was proposing to her, unable to remember what those allusions were intended to arouse since she had buried it beneath layers and layers of inaccessible and blessed oblivion. But Costa refused to admit defeat and one night he arrived at the cabin, a little tipsy as well, like someone whom La Violadita and Waldo had once known and who, some time ago now, had returned, naked and nameless, to the earth, which, as if he had been a worm, had fed him, urged him with false promises to spend a somnolent period on its surface, and finally had swallowed him up again. Costa began to struggle with La Violadita, and Waldo, who was watching them as he sucked on a sweet, started shaking his hands joined over his chest and murmuring more and more rapidly, with a diction that would have been perfect had it not been for his mania for making the saliva hiss between his teeth, "Costa, abusing his command, by month's end will not be on hand, Costa abusing his command, by month's end will not be on hand," more rapidly and more loudly each time, to the point that Costa, who was counting on Waldo's muteness so that what he had in mind to do would not be divulged and who considered him so unimportant that he had even thought of doing it in his presence, let go of La Violadita and began to move backwards toward the door of the cabin, so terrified by the sounds coming out of Waldo's mouth, whose meaning he didn't understand in the least, which was all the better for him, since if he had understood it, he would have been even more terrified. Two weeks later, dead drunk, Costa fell off his horse and was killed.

Waldo not only spoke, but spoke in verse and only in verse, in octosyllables, forming rhymed couplets that he repeated several times in a row, nodding his head slightly, and making his saliva hiss between his teeth. But he was stingy with them; only very infrequently did he consent to give out with them, and always only if La Violadita asked him to, and at times only in exchange for a sweet or some other treat as well. The village priest shook his head, annoyed by this revelation, which introduced complications into what he thought about those two creatures who had cropped up on the pampas and whom he, out of compassion, had taken in one morning in the brick portico of the chapel. And above all because, in the same mysterious way in which everyone knew what had happened between La Violadita and her father, everybody knew immediately that Waldo spoke in verse, and that he had prophesied Costa's death. In the beginning, they began to look at him with curiosity rather than with respect, finding it hard to believe that that chubby little nine-year-old halfbreed was capable of predicting events, but doubt rather than conviction is more frequently what forges reputations, and it suffices for that doubt to perceive in the real a shadow, or the illusion of a shadow of refutation, for it to transform itself overnight into conviction. One morning, a couple of months later, Waldo and La Violadita were crossing through the hamlet, heading toward the church, she in front, with her starched little white dress, he behind, giving little leaps in the air and continually nodding his head, in his habitual sign of assent, when suddenly he stopped, and began to repeat, almost without opening his mouth, between his teeth that made his saliva hiss: "I saw a bird up in the sky, burning like fire as it flew by, I saw a bird up in the sky, burning like fire as it flew by," so that La Violadita grabbed him by the hand, and running so fast that Waldo could scarcely keep up with her with his little rigid steps, went to tell the priest what had happened. That night, some roaming Indians attacked the village, but Waldo's couplet had alerted the inhabitants, and even though nobody knew what it meant, the attack did not take them by surprise, and the following morning the dozen Indians in rags, who had been trying to get themselves some horses and some white women to enliven their existence during their monotonous wanderings on the pampas, lay riddled with bullets in a pond on the outskirts of the village.

The people of the village began to seek prophecies from him, to want him to tell them what neither they nor anyone else could anticipate, synthesized in one of those octosyllabic couplets which, to tell the truth, were often as impenetrable as the future that they seemed to fathom, but which to those who listened to them gave them the impression of being a projectile that time was sending to them from the future, and which pierced the transparent wall of the present, like a message tied to a stone pierces the glass pane of a window. At first, when they came to see him, to ask him things, Waldo remained mute, absent, entrenched in his perpetual assent, but when they began to bring him sweets, caramels, a few banknotes easy to exchange for lollipops or chocolate, he deigned to accelerate the nods of his head, to make his saliva hiss through his teeth even more loudly, and to come out with his perfect couplets, with lilting rhythms and even better rhymes, repeating them several times in a frenetic crescendo that made his wide, dark face, flattened like a toad's, grow slightly paler, and that, obliging him to move his lips, caused him to reveal his big white horse teeth, until all of a sudden he fell silent, though for some time he went on moving his lips, which he never closed altogether, as though the bones of his face were too wide for the skin covering them. After a year, an old woman maintained that she had seen him hovering half a meter above the floor, and the people of the village would cross themselves when they saw him pass by, his face a blank, indifferent to his reputation, giving little leaps in the air behind La Violadita and perpetually nodding his head. One day, some soldiers from Río Cuarto arrived, wanting him to go back there with them to bless a regiment, so that people saw the two of them, Waldo and La Violadita, on horseback, crossing the pampas at a slow pace, with their escort of soldiers and a recruit who rode alongside them the whole time so as to protect them from the sun with a parasol.

They began to be a familiar element of the landscape, beneath the sky filled with clouds to the point of ostentation or empty from one end of the horizon to the other, on the shores of the ponds where pink flamingos and teros and little birds were no longer startled on seeing them pass by, in patches of thistles so high that Waldo, astride his pony, grimaced in annoyance when they tickled his face as they went by, tiny creatures, almost nonexistent on the pampas, she all in white and he in a brand-new gaucho outfit, straight out of an operetta, wide and stiff, ceaselessly moving his lips that never completely covered his teeth, with a round, narrow-brimmed sombrero pushed back a little from his forehead, a short black embroidered vest and a pair of black balloon trousers so wide that their drooping pleats almost entirely covered his gleaming boots. They were summonsed everywhere, and they crossed the countryside in all directions, beyond Buenos Aires, as far as the environs of Córdoba, in the precarious settlements that were forming on the flat surface of the oldest land in the world, covered by the sediment of continents and of extinct species and pulverized by time and the harsh weather, that unreal and empty space that the conquistadors took special care to avoid but that, the Indians first, then later cows and horses, and shortly thereafter adventurers, soldiers and landowners, and then later still the disinherited of the whole world who had arrived in overcrowded ships, stubbornly persisted in crossing again and again, gray, hallucinated figures, leaving fleeting traces that the strong winds and the rain undertook almost immediately to efface. They were like a mocking persistence which, unwittingly defying the cosmic mill that had provided this bare plain as an example of what awaited other continents, supposedly majestic mountain peaks and their illusively eternal snows, greedy species in presumed evolution, traversed in passing the desolate fields, a persistence so deeply etched within them after a few years had gone by that even the Indians, who at the time, having risen in revolt against the whites, spent their days slitting throats or getting their own slit, watched them from a distance with apprehension, with emotion almost, and let them go on their way.

One day when they were back in Coronda, one of the sisters, the only one left in the family, who had been working in a brothel in Buenos Aires till she caught herself a retired sergeant and married him, appeared in the village. The sergeant had been given a discharge from the Army because he had lost an arm in Paraguay. He had a bit of education and with the pension they'd given him, plus the savings that his wife had made from working in the brothel, he planned to set up a small business. But when he learned of Waldo's gift, it seemed to him that destiny was demanding of him that he prove his talents as an organizer and impresario. In a few days, Waldo and La Violadita adored the sergeant. He never came back to the village without sweets or garlands to decorate the altars that La Violadita had set up in the cabins they had lived in, with little religious prints, statues, embroidered altar cloths, paper flowers that she made herself, rosaries and candelabra. And when they went off traveling somewhere, he himself rode alongside them with the parasol. Sometimes he arrived in a village before them, and to drum up people's interest, he did a little advertising; he went to see the village priest, the justice of the peace, the chief of police, taking a little present, a little money, assuring them that they were on the side of order and the Church, that Waldo had seen Baby Jesus several times; he had a leaflet printed that he handed out to the public – quite useless, in fact, since most of the villagers were illiterate – in which the major prophecies of Waldo and three or four miracles attributed to him were described. When people came to see Waldo, the sergeant made them form a line, and standing next to Waldo, before they could consult him, he collected the money or gifts that they were bringing to him and made them move on at a brisk pace. They passed by Waldo, who murmured his couplet with his eye on the packets of sweets that his brother-in-law was piling up on a little table, and then they were ushered out by La Violadita and her sister.

One night when Waldo was drowsing, his body rigid on his cot, the sergeant pushed his sombrero back with the damp, gnawed end of the dead cigar that he was holding between the fingers of his only hand, and declared:

"The countryside is fine, but it's already been milked dry. Today it's necessary to go work in the cities."

"They don't even leave us in peace in the morning," Gina says, waving her hand in front of her face in order to chase away the cloud of mosquitoes that is hovering around her.

Bianco, who has just appeared in the doorway of the study, ready to go out, wearing an iridescent lilac-colored jacket and pale-green checkered trousers, stops at the end of the porch and looks at her; in the eight and a half months of her pregnancy, Gina has put on at least thirty pounds, and sitting in the wicker armchair, on the edge of the porch opposite, so as to take better advantage of the occasional puffs of breeze and yet remain sheltered from the April sun, abnormally strong and unhealthful, she has the impassivity and the vague form of a pyramid, with the lower part of her body sunk down into the armchair, and the upper part, that grows narrower and narrower, crowned by a circular, glistening chignon into which the hair atop her head has been pulled taut. An ample dress, of a yellowish orange, swells in three places despite a generous cut, two of them on her breasts and one, a more prominent bulge, at the level of her lower belly, while her arms, which emerge, plump and matte, from the armholes in her sleeveless dress, show a number of folds a little below her armpits, and between her shoulders and her elbows; her cheeks descend, in an unbroken line that effaces the contours of her jaws, down to her double chin; the straight open neckline of her dress, generously low-cut so as to relieve her continual fatigue with a bit of coolness, shows the great dark, glistening bulk of her breasts, which, because of the tight fit of the bodice, unable to hold them in, press together and rise a little, forming two parentheses that meet at the tops of their respective curves and are prolonged beneath the fabric.

"Don't expose yourself like that," Bianco says, running his hand through his brick-colored hair to check that it is properly groomed.

"They're everywhere," Gina says, sighing and fanning herself with her hand, listlessly and distractedly, apparently certain that, however hard she tries, she will get no relief from either the heat or the mosquitoes.

"Shall I wait for you for lunch?" she asks after a few seconds' silence.

"I imagine so," Bianco says, and as he begins crossing the patio toward her, he goes on: "It's a strictly professional visit. I want to have a look at him at first hand to see if he's as good as his reputation makes him out to be."

When he reaches her wicker chair, he bends down toward her and brushes her cheeks with his lips. He is on the point of straightening up again, but Gina holds him back by the lapel of his iridescent jacket, and sniffs him two or three times before letting go of him.

"Cognac at eleven in the morning?" she says to him reproachfully.

"I slept badly last night," Bianco says. "It's a liqueur. It gets me off on the right foot for the rest of the day."

Gina bursts out laughing. In the months that have gone by and gradually changed the shape of her body, and even her manner of existence, making her more detached, more distant and more placid, only the unfathomable frankness of her eyes, whose true meaning forever escapes him, has remained unchanged, and as time has passed, Bianco, frequently beset by dark, uncontrollable thoughts, feels less capable of withstanding her gaze.

"Pretexts," Gina says. And then, looking him over from head to foot: "What elegance."

With a considerable effort, Bianco manages to smile; in the first place, Gina's intimate insolence, her mocking manner whereby she seems to refute, in an apparently jovial way, his explanation concerning the cognac, irritates him slightly, making him feel not very highly respected, as is also true of the allusion to his attire, in which Gina has subtly implied that Bianco might be going somewhere else than to a professional meeting, an amorous rendezvous, for example, which seems to him to reveal in Gina an omnipresent concupiscence of which she may not even be aware, and for that very reason seems much more intolerable to Bianco. Instead of answering, his face still set in a forced smile, he shrugs in order to minimize his supposed elegance.

He goes out into the street, where his horse, already saddled, tethered to a post on the edge of the sidewalk, is waiting for him, indifferent and serene. He mounts it in one leap and trots along, tense and lost in thought. The sudden heat, after a fleeting sign of autumn has established an indecision in the atmosphere, and the leaves of the trees, that have been wilting in the tremendous heat waves and yellowing as autumn arrived, reveal, by their sparseness and their faded colors, their reddish or yellowish tips, the incongruity of the morning sun, its heat still intense but its light growing less strong. The cognac boils in Bianco's brain, as he sees, from astride his horse, a horizon that has retreated, toward which the vacant lots, the vegetable gardens, the scattered houses, the trees, the badly designed streets of sandy earth lying between the grass growing in the ditches and in the cracks of the almost nonexistent sidewalks, as they fade from sight in vanishing perspective, become immersed in a denser and denser haze of sultry heat, which, although it is transparent enough not to conceal them completely, by blurring their contours some-what and making their volumes vague and fuzzy, confers on them a sort of unreality. The old, long-established families live in the south of the city, the nouveaux riches in the north, allowing everyone else to share the other directions of space, in accordance with the random possibilities that chance offers them, including the far south and the far north, in which, from a dividing line beyond which space ceases to be consecrated by the presence of the rich, anyone can establish himself if he has sufficient means to buy or rent a part of this space from those very same rich, who even though they do not regard these areas as fit to live in none the less continue to own them. Hence Bianco must ride through very nearly the entire city, skirting the river's edge at one moment in order to arrive at his destination; after he has ridden along for a good while, the houses begin to be more frequent, the streets better laid out between the ditches, until the horse's shoes begin to resound on paving stones and Bianco must pass through the heart of the city where old colonial houses with thick adobe walls and Spanish roof tiles often share a party wall with other more modern houses, includ-ing a number that are several stories high, many of them of unplastered brick, with irregular brick sidewalks, and bitter orange, chinaberry, rubber, jacaranda and silk-cotton trees growing along the edges, in the back patios or in the public squares. At this hour in the morning, itinerant peddlers are hawking their wares, and loafers are having idle conversations together on the sidewalks, under the trees, smoking a cigar and chasing away with one resigned hand the clouds of mosquitoes flying up from the ditches. Bianco leaves the center of the city behind and begins to trot once again down streets of sandy earth until he stops in front of a large cabin painted white, and with-out dismounting from his horse, attentively observes what is going on near the entrance. The sergeant, with the empty right sleeve of his shirt folded in two, held down at the height of his shoulder with a safety pin, is making ostentatious gestures with his one arm, holding a cigar that has gone out between two fingers, addressing some twenty people who are in the front patio, vainly trying to get closer to the door or look through the crack or through the rectangle of the window covered by a cretonne curtain, so as to catch a glimpse of the inside of the cabin.

"I've already told you that he can't see you today. Not before day after tomorrow," the sergeant says, with amiable authority, to those who seem to be insisting that he let them inside the cabin. Some of them, who look as though they are sick, are being held upright by members of their family, others have a hen or a little package under their arm, others show the sergeant, in an effort to persuade him, two or three banknotes, which the sergeant refuses with a dignified but jovial air, so as to show that it is not a question of money but of a real obstacle that, if it were in his power, for the good of all those who are pestering him, he would have immediately eliminated. The sergeant raises his head and sees Bianco, who is looking down at him from astride his horse, and greets him with a wave of his hand and a broad, welcoming smile, but as Bianco is about to dismount, he shakes his head, and making a circular motion with his one good hand and moving his right shoulder on which the empty shirt sleeve attached with the safety pin quivers a little, indicates to him that he should go around the side of the cabin to the back patio. "It's the Versailles of cabins," Bianco thinks, observing the building which, made of adobe bricks all the same size and well tamped down into thick walls, a well-cut thatched roof and regular openings with real wooden frames, has been recently whitewashed and gleams in the morning light. At the back, there are a well-cared-for vegetable garden and a flower garden, and still farther back a cart whose shafts are resting on the ground, three or four horses, and a henhouse. There is thick shade from the trees too, but their foliage, already attacked by autumn, dappled with red, yellow, brown, allows the sun's rays to pass through its gaps, which will go on increasing in size in the coming days. Bianco gets down from his horse and ties the bridle to a tree trunk, just as the sergeant joins him in the back patio.

"A pleasure to see you," the sergeant says. As he holds his left hand out to him, Bianco hesitates a little, not knowing which of his own hands to offer him, until, deciding in favor of the right one, he gives the sergeant a slightly awkward, clumsy handshake, and at the same time, because of the posture that the two of them must assume, one burdened with a sensation of excessive familiarity.

"Waldo is waiting for you," the sergeant says, seemingly about to go inside the cabin.

"Wait. Here," Bianco says, putting his hand in his pocket and taking out a packet of banknotes.

"No, no," the sergeant says. "Give them to his sister, right in front of him. He likes to see the banknotes. I do all this because I'm one of the family. And because I believe in him."

Bianco follows him inside. Although the morning light is coming through the door and through the windows despite the cretonne curtains, in the first room there are many lighted candles, in tin or wooden candelabra, on saucers, on little round bases of wood floating in basins or large platters, illuminating images and little statues of saints fastened to the wall or leaning on shelves covered by embroidered runners made of an immaculate white cloth. The sergeant appears proud of the decoration and observes Bianco to study his reaction, but Bianco allows his eyes to wander indifferently, almost scornfully, around the room, and walking resolutely on, stops only when he reaches the cretonne curtain that separates them from the next room.

"Go right on in," the sergeant says, and takes a few steps ahead of him so as to pull the curtain aside.

Bianco goes through the empty space left by the curtain when it was pulled back and enters the room: the halfbreed Waldo is sitting on a chair with a straw seat in the middle of the room and La Violadita, dressed in white, standing next to him, delicately leaning her hand on the edge of the back of his chair, appears to concentrate in herself alone the outward perception of both of them, for she alone directs her gaze toward Bianco when he enters the room. Waldo, turned in the direction precisely opposite the door through which Bianco has just come into the room, keeps nodding his head continually and is holding by the very end of its little wooden stick a round lollipop, consisting of a substance with oblique white and red stripes which is already slightly transparent from being licked and which Waldo slowly raises to his mouth, without putting it inside, but instead sticking out his broad tongue, stained white and red from the lollipop, which licks its white and red surface, slowly, meticulously, efficiently, and then gets put back inside Waldo's mouth as he entrenches it behind his big white horse teeth, which his mouth, whose lips move constantly, does not completely cover, as though the skin of his face were too small in relation to his jawbone.

"Come in, come in, sir," La Violadita says. "The poor little thing likes sweets a lot. He's happy today. He slept well."

"Thank you," Bianco says.

When he first heard about Waldo, a couple of years back, from a doctor who had been present at one of Waldo's appearances near Esperanza, Bianco was so fascinated that he planned a trip to Coronda, and once, going overland to Buenos Aires, he stopped in the village to go visit him, but the priest, in whose house he stayed overnight and with whom he had a long conversation, informed him that Waldo and his sister were out on the road, somewhere around Córdoba. When he learned the week before that Waldo had just settled down for a stay in the city, he sent word to the sergeant, who he had been told took care of Waldo and his sister, to propose to him the special visit, not with the aim of asking him for a prophecy, but merely to observe Waldo and in order to reassure the sergeant, who apparently was afraid of a conspiracy similar to the one that he, Bianco, had had to endure at the hands of the positivists seven years before in Paris, Bianco held out a silver spoon to him, telling him to keep a tight grip on one end of it, and then, gently passing the index and middle fingers of his left hand over the spoon for a couple of minutes, barely touching it, had made it bend in two as though it were made of soft clay. "Ah, a colleague," the sergeant said with respectful admiration, and casting a glance around Bianco's study, where the latter had received him, he thought that Bianco was a useful contact to have, one whom, if one took into account the house he lived in, he had a great deal to learn from.

Bianco steps forward a few paces and halts a couple of meters away from the brother and sister, keeping a certain distance away the better to observe them. Plump, dark-skinned, staring blankly into space, Waldo appears to ignore his presence completely, and Bianco marvels at the perfect stability of his narrow-brimmed sombrero, pushed back a little way off his forehead, despite the perpetual nodding of his head. His hand holding the lollipop has remained up close to his mouth, and separating his upper and lower teeth, Waldo sticks his tongue out again, slowly, conscientiously licking with pleasure the circular surface divided into oblique white and red stripes, and Bianco has the impression that this chubby bulk, carefully dressed in its Sunday best, an embroidered vest and black silk balloon trousers, is a sort of automaton that works by means of a very complicated inner mechanism whose rare outward gestures, slow and repetitive, do not manage to give a spectator any idea of the multiple hidden gears that make it possible for them to be performed. Meanwhile, La Violadita appears to be devotedly taking care of him, serious and proud, but at the same time on the alert, as though it were her responsibility, by redoubling her own vigilance, to pay the price of indifference toward the outside world that her brother seems to flaunt. Bianco puts his hand in his pocket, takes out a number of banknotes, folds them in two and hands them to her; she takes them without counting them, without even looking at them, and leans the hand that she is grasping them in against the white fabric of her dress, at the level of her belly. Without even moving his head, turned continuously in a direction just to one side of Bianco, Waldo appears to have noticed the banknotes since, lowering the hand that is holding the lollipop up, he begins to make the saliva hiss between his white teeth, and to move his lips, especially the corners of them, in a faster rhythm, giving the impression that the inner mechanism governing his movements has speeded up. The skin of his face, too dark to grow flushed, seems on the contrary to lighten a little, to turn gray, through a sort of effort that he gives signs of making, or that in any event is betrayed by the more and more rapid movement of his head and the more intense hissing sounds of his saliva between his teeth, to the point that a few little drops of foam spatter his pale, taut lips. A noise begins to build up in his throat and Bianco, who speaks so many languages with the same foreign accent, knows that that noise is not the embryo of any known language, that it is prior to words and if it is true that that dark and spongy mass of flesh piled up in the chair has the gift of prophecy, that gift does not come to him from words, but rather, traveling through unknown, tortuous tunnels of time, of energy, and of matter bent to his will, going and coming through them without his moving from his chair with the straw seat, the noise will condescend for a few instants to be imperfectly decanted into words that will be, for him, without exception, foreign. And the words begin to come out, laboriously, from between his clenched teeth wet with saliva. They form two perfect rhymed octosyllables that are repeated again and again, in a voice that becomes higher and higher and more and more tremulous: "A cloud is aborning, sister, certain to darken the morning, A cloud is aborning, sister, certain to darken the morning," in a more and more frenetic crescendo which, when it reaches its paroxysm, stops abruptly, although the same is not true of the movements of his lips, the hisses of saliva and the acquiescent nodding of his head, that gradually lessen until they take on their usual rhythm of before the crisis, and as if the entire mechanism that governs the spongy mass dressed to the nines wished to inform Bianco that the demonstration was now over, the hand holding the lollipop slowly rises to the level of his mouth and his broad tongue emerges from between his teeth and begins to lick the circle of oblique white and red stripes, so transparent now because of his effective licking that Bianco can even glimpse the little stick buried in the cloyingly sweet, crystalline substance.

"What did you think of it?" the sergeant asks him, as Bianco unties the horse's bridle, in the back patio, and prepares to climb into the saddle.

"Very interesting," Bianco says. "I'll come back again."

"Did you hear what he said?" the sergeant asks.

"Yes. I heard," Bianco says. And he thinks: "If he's a fraud, he's no doubt one of the best. But nobody can be a fraud who looks like that."

"Upsetting," the sergeant says.

Bianco doesn't answer him. He is about to shake his hand to say goodbye, but remembering the complication that this act entails, he prefers to abstain from going through with it, and hearing the murmur of the people waiting near the main entrance, in the front patio, he decides to walk to the street. The sergeant accompanies him, respectfully; he appears to have interpreted Bianco's decision not to shake his hand as a gesture of tact.

"'Well," the sergeant says. "I must go convince those people that they'll have to come back day after tomorrow. Goodbye and good luck."

"Thank you," Bianco says. Leading the horse by the bridle, he heads for the street. A voice calling to him in Italian brings him up short.

"Ilustrissimo. Ilustrissimo," the voice says.

From among the group of those who are waiting in front of the door, a man hurriedly approaches him and respectfully removing his sombrero, so that he already is holding it in his hand by the time he has almost caught up with Bianco, stops a short distance away in order to show his deference. Between his salt-and-pepper beard and his gray hair, his eyes are smiling, timid and respectful.

"How are you, ilustrissimo? Do you remember me?"

Bianco looks closely at him for quite a while, knowing that his face is familiar, but fails to recognize him.

"Calabria. The boat," the man says, with a smile meant to prompt Bianco to recognize him, after giving him two or three broad hints. Bianco makes such an eloquent gesture, raising his arms in the air, that the horse, behind him, gives a little start and shakes its head, giving a feeble neigh.

"Of course I remember," Bianco says in Italian. "We also met in Buenos Aires, do you recall?"

"Of course. You treated me so kindly, ilustrissimo," the man says, twirling his sombrero by the brim with the ends of his fingers, holding it against his belly.

"And how have things gone with you?" Bianco asks.

The Calabrian shrugs: not all that well, he says in Italian. He has never been able to obtain the title deeds to his land; he has sown crops, true enough, and harvested them, but as a share-cropper. And, he says, he is in the same straits as the day he arrived.

"And what about your family?" Bianco asks.

The Calabrian makes a vague movement with his head, indicating an indeterminate direction in space.

"In Italy," he says. "We couldn't make a go of it here. I send them part of what I earn." Then he holds his hat in one hand and pressing the fingers of his free hand together into a fist, leaving only his thumb sticking out, he points with it several times over his shoulder. "Did you see him?" he asks.

"Yes. But he's not receiving people till day after tomorrow," Bianco says.

"I don't know what to do now, whether to go back to Italy, or stay here, or bring my family over. I don't know. That's why I've come to consult him," the Calabrian says.

"It's a good idea. You've nothing to lose," Bianco says.

"And what did he tell you?" the Calabrian asks.

"I didn't come to consult him," Bianco says. "I came to study him. So as to..." – and raising his hand in the air, as though he had an imaginary pen between his fingers, he gestures as if he were writing.

"Ah, I understand," the Calabrian says, rather impressed.

Bianco puts his hand in his pocket, and without taking out the packet of banknotes, peels off two or three bills from it and hands them to him.

"No, please, ilustrissimo," the man says, lowering his head a little.

"Yes, yes," Bianco says. "Buy him some sweets. He's fond of sweets."

The Calabrian steals a glance at the group of people on the

front patio to make sure that nobody is watching, and quickly taking the bills immediately tucks them out of sight in his pocket.

"Thanks, ilustrissimo," the Calabrian says.

"Do you know how to put up wire fencing?" Bianco says. "I'm fencing my lands in and I need workers. People who come from around here don't know how to do it."

"They're a bunch of morons," the Calabrian says. "Except for wielding a knife, they're no good at anything."

"If you stay, come and see me," Bianco says.

"If I stay," the Calabrian says, almost apologetically. "I've just enough for my return passage. Let me see what the halfbreed tells me. Whatever he tells me, I'll do it."

"Buy him some sweets," Bianco says.

They bid each other goodbye. The Calabrian heads back toward the cabin and Bianco mounts his horse. Impatient because of the wait that Bianco has subjected it to, having a talk with the sergeant first, and then with the Calabrian in front of the cabin, the horse wants to take off at a gallop, so that Bianco must rein him in, and in the struggle to keep his mount under control, which lasts for a hundred yards or so, Bianco holds the reins taut and the animal goes forward one nervous little step at a time, veering off a little to one side and trembling slightly at having to hold back. But Bianco feels like riding along slowly so as to free his attention and reflect on what he has seen inside the cabin, and finally, relaxing a little from the tension of being held back as it advances along the sandy street, the animal calms down and allows itself to be calmly led along at a walk by its rider. Instead of dispersing, the fog that blurs the horizon remains as it was, despite the sun which is already at the zenith and which, with its vertical light, of anachronistic intensity, seems to flatten the houses that are already flat, rectangular and graceless, becoming more frequent as Bianco approaches the center of the city. There is not a breath of air and in the trees, motionless and drooping almost lifelessly, the foliage, contaminated by reddish, yellowish and brown spots, gives the impression that it could fall off altogether at the slightest shake. "It is neither autumn nor summer," Bianco thinks. "It doesn't resemble any season at all; it's like a corpse of summer already rotting away and there is no way of knowing what it's going to end up as." It is true that, for some months now, his thoughts have been like the leaves of the trees, stained with a rust that bleeds onto them or by which they appear to become impregnated, like a piece of metal long buried in the bottom of a swamp, where unknown organic substances had begun to dissolve it, so that the rarefied, murky air that goes in and out of his lungs, the fog on the horizon and his confused and hazy emotions, the morning light, misleadingly bright, and the evidence with which it seems to him that he perceives the outside world, may be a single fluid, a homogeneous current of which the inner and the outer are no more than the two uncertain and fluctuating extremes. Abruptly, without knowing why, Bianco begins to feel the palpitation that is an alarm signal at the nape of his neck and in his back, between the shoulder blades, and moving his head in all directions, surprised and attentive, trying to discover the cause of his excitement, until, after a few seconds of floating in a vague place, in a time without dimensions, deprived of self-consciousness or identity, as though he had fallen into a brief faint, he realizes that his horse is proceeding at a walk down the street where Garay López's house is located and that something, an event that has just taken place during his extremely short loss of self-awareness, a sudden shock that has occurred in the outside world but has been intense enough to give him a bad jolt at a distance, has just transpired in the street, so that by keeping his head rigid, pretending to raise his eyes and rivet them on the horizon in order not to give himself away, he directs his gaze toward the entrance of the house just in time to see Garay López, or someone who closely resembles him, appear in the entrance, perceive him, Bianco, coming on horseback down the middle of the street, deserted because it is past midday, stop abruptly on seeing him, and hurriedly go back into the house so as not to be taken by surprise in return. "He can't have aged that much in a few months," Bianco thinks, and for a few seconds he tells himself that he has thought so much about Garay López that he has just had a hallucination; that by dint of being so eager for Garay López to come to the city after receiving his letter, the supreme recourse for disentangling the knot of shadow and substance that has been stifling him ever since he came back from the country and found Gina puffing on a cigar with an expression of intense pleasure, a missive that he had sent to Garay López the week before so as to force him to place the evidence within his reach, has brought into the light of day, as someone throws a stone in the air to unburden himself of his impatience, the image of his desire in order to drive away something close to madness. But when he rides down the middle of the street past the door, he tries to look in the direction of the house out of the corner of his eye and it seems to him that he sees, through the door open just a crack, that someone is watching him from inside. But he is not certain that it is Garay López; the figure that he has seen appear for a fraction of a second and then hurriedly turn around and go back into the house to hide behind the door and whose reality Bianco no longer doubts in the least, might have been identical to Garay López, a little older, admittedly, but above all what differentiates him from Garay López is the obvious untidiness of his attire, dirty and wrinkled, and his complexion: the man whom he has seen in the doorway has a head of straight hair and a beard that are coal-black, but instead of the pale oval face that they ordinarily frame, Bianco has seen a bright pink, flushed face, and his elongated features looked rounder to him, puffy almost, as though he hadn't slept. "Maybe he's drunk," Bianco thinks, "he too needs a little pick-me-up of cognac at eleven in the morning to endure the waiting, and he's going to go on drinking as long as he doesn't know whether the live thing that's going to come out all bloody and howling from between Gina's legs has hair that's straight and black or brick-red like mine." Bianco clenches his teeth and half-opening his lips in a bitter grimace, so that a few drops of sweat slide down his upper lip and slip into his mouth, and lashing the horse's neck with the end of the reins, he sets it to galloping down the deserted street.

When he arrives home, covered with sweat, he leaps down from the horse and stands motionless in the street for a moment, suddenly reflective, after the ride at a gallop, during which, at the same time as the flaccid masses of his body, the horse's movements have seemed to jolt as well the images rushing headlong into and out of the clear part of his mind, colliding and superimposing themselves on each other at so great a speed that they have appeared to be emerging from somewhere even more remote than his own innermost depths, strange, incomprehensible and alien, to the point that for a few seconds he has had a picture of himself, Bianco, as though he were someone else, someone that he has known in other times, in other places, buried forever, in a hazy zone, that has swallowed up not only the first thirty years of his life, but the entire past, curds of disintegrating matter vanishing into nothingness. But now that he is standing alongside the palpitating, panting horse beneath the foliage of red, yellow and brown of the trees that are standing, wilting, along the edge of the sidewalk, now that he knows that he will be obliged to sit down across from Gina and eat with her, to confront her oddly frank and unfathomable gaze, as he waits for the inner images that have been badly shaken up during the gallop return to the calm order of that morning, he begins to tell himself, as though he were talking with someone else, trying to make him see reason, to convince him with irrefutable arguments: "Calm down, Bianco, if he was the one who was in the doorway, and we're certain that it was him, that it couldn't have been anybody but him, getting sloshed to the gills with cognac from mid-morning on, ever since the day he received my letter, if it was him, and there's no question that it was him, it is Bianco who controls reality, he who reigns over the movements of the larvae of what is secondary, over the excremental order, it is Bianco who plans, by the force of the mind alone, by a calculated act of will, the events of the world, he and not those who, unwittingly possessed by bloody and sardonic forces, whose very existence they know nothing of, let alone their existence in their very own selves, abandon themselves to what they think is a pleasure and in reality is nothing but a chemical accident and disintegration." And looking at the hand that is holding the reins, the back of it covered with a sparse, brick-colored down, he continues to stare at it until it stops trembling.

"He doesn't appear to be a fraud," he says to Gina at the table, as he serves himself from the platter that the maid presents to him, hurrying a bit since Gina, who has served herself first, is waiting for him so as to start eating – "no, not in the least. He lacks the intelligence to be a con man. But as for taking his stammerings to be a prophecy.... In a word, the subject would have to be studied in more detail."

"I'd like to wash myself after my nap," Gina says, as though she hasn't been listening to Bianco.

Repressing his annoyance at Gina's lack of attention, so frequent since their marriage that he has finally ended up regarding it as a sort of mania, Bianco answers amiably:

"I'll help you."

"Yes, I prefer that." And noticing that the maid has disappeared in the direction of the kitchen, she adds, lowering her voice a little: "I don't want to show too much of myself in this condition."

"I understand perfectly," Bianco says.

Because of the heat, Gina has decided that they would have lunch on the porch, seeking, so as to relieve her feeling of suffocation a little, the illusory drafts of cool air that stubbornly refuse to blow, and in all truth it might have been a little cooler in the dining room, but incapable of contradicting her, Bianco pretends that the porches are the coolest spot in the house these days, a fact belied by the light of the sun that beats straight down onto the rectangular patio, heating the air on the porches that are in the shade.

"I'd like to know how it all began. The sergeant says it happened all of a sudden, that until he was nine years old he hadn't said one word and that, from one day to the next, he started speaking in verse," Bianco says. "If it isn't any sort of trick, it's quite amazing. But if it's a fraud, I wonder how they go about it. Perhaps the sister and the sergeant compose the verses and make him learn them by heart."

"Why would there necessarily be any trickery?" Gina says. "When we do our own experiments, is there any sort of trickery involved?"

Bianco raises his eyes from his plate and looks at her. In her fleshy, matte face, in which her cheeks join her double chin to form a single mass of smooth flesh, her eyes, open wide, take up a great deal of space, and their gaze is so steady, full of such perfect sincerity that it begins to upset Bianco to the point that he lowers his head toward his plate again.

"No. Of course not," Bianco answers.

As Gina takes her afternoon nap, Bianco shuts himself up in the study with the bottle of cognac, and leaning his neck on the edge of the back of the sofa, sits there looking at the white surface of the ceiling, as he slowly turns the glass between his hands, in a calm reverie, or an empty one rather, caught up again in that sort of cold discouragement that attacks him when, prevented by events from going into action, he finds himself obliged to wait until, obeying his predictions step by step, the real manifests itself. Finally, for quite some time, he loses himself in the white surface, in the infinite shades of white that it seems to him he can discern in it, in white turbulences, in white spirals against a white background, in concentric circles that revolve in several directions at once, in white volutes that take on relief and stand out from the surface, creating a series of organic leaps and starts as though the ceiling were a well of quicklime. He allows himself to become so spellbound by the white labyrinth that it is only when Gina knocks on the door for the third time that he hears, and leaping to his feet in one bound, so abruptly that part of the cognac spills on his trousers, he begins to head for the door just as Gina opens it and comes inside the study.

"Were you asleep?" Gina asks.

"No. I was thinking," Bianco says.

Gina takes the glass of cognac out of his hands.

"I'm beginning to know you," she says. "Something's bothering you."

"Me?" Bianco asks.

And he shakes his head.

"So much the better," Gina says, and burying her long fingers in the thick curls of his brick-colored hair, stuck together a little from sweat, she strokes them for a moment. Bianco feels crushed by the imposing presence of Gina who, gently taking hold of him by the shoulder, takes him with her to the bathroom. There is a big empty tub on the mosaic tile floor, and two or three containers of warm water already prepared. Gina gets undressed and gets into the empty tub, standing in the center of it, and holding out her arm and moving all her fingers impatiently, her mind elsewhere, points out to Bianco a tin pitcher floating in one of the big vessels full of water.

"I can't even bend over any more," Gina says.

"What do you think I'm here for?" Bianco replies. He leans over to fill the pitcher of water and as he straightens up again, he comes closer to Gina to hand her the pitcher, with his head turned a little to one side and his eyes lowered, as though he didn't dare look at her, as though he were afraid that her heavy, abundant flesh might secrete some deadly fluid. Her arms, her neck, her legs, her breasts, her buttocks, her belly have swollen so much that her flesh, stretched to its maximum tautness, gleams, having become a little smoother and a little lighter in color, as though the pigmentation of her skin had been diluted and there where the flesh is more supple circular folds so deep have formed that her skin gives the impression that the flesh underneath the folds of fat has been tied together with an invisible wire. On her round belly, over whose upper part her swollen breasts droop, their dark nipples almost disappearing, her navel stands out like a hard polyp, and the strip of curving black down disappears beneath her belly that almost completely hides the hair of her pubis.

"Wait a minute, please," Gina says. And raising her arms, she begins to let her hair down. Because of her position, of the movement of her hands that linger to undo the knots in her hair, her entire body ebbs and flows with slow undulations, which are repeated periodically each time her hands perform the same fruitless motions, and when her hands get impatient because they have encountered some difficulty and their gestures become more violent, the undulations grow more rapid and more intense, transmitting themselves to her neck which becomes full of folds, to her breasts which sway back and forth, to her belly which trembles, to her arms on which the skin quivers, and to her feet that move a little on the bottom of the tub. Finally Gina manages to do what she has set out to do and her hair falls in a black shower down her back, shaking from the fall, with the ends curled up slightly because of the topknot that held them imprisoned, and after having tossed it slowly, energetically across her shoulders, Gina takes the pitcher that Bianco is holding out to her and pours the water over her face, closing her eyes from the impact and holding the pitcher out blindly to Bianco for him to fill it again. They repeat the operation several times, and then, slowly and carefully, Gina soaps herself. Bianco scrubs her back and then he begins to rinse her off, gently pouring over her, one after another, the pitchers full of warm water. Finally he kneels down on the floor and soaps her legs and feet. At one point he raises his head and looks at her: from below, Gina seems enormous, almost infinite to him, towering upward in circles of flesh that form a vast pyramid whose summit, thinning out to a finer and finer point, seems to disappear gradually in the semidarkness of the ceiling. And when, still on his knees, he straightens up a little, positioning himself in front of her so as to soap the front of her thighs, his face remains almost glued to her incredibly tense, round belly, and for a few seconds it seems to him that he perceives, from the other side of her skin, of the hard protuberance of her navel, of the curved strip of black down hidden by the outer edge of this sphere, the magma of matter in action, churning in limitless combinations and transformations, the motley pools of substance colliding and intermingling, without any other purpose than that constant fabrication of humors, of tissues, of repetitive, transitory, monotonous, inhuman concretions, the four or five variations of the same adverse sound, persistent and meaningless.

Then he helps her to get dressed, leaves her in the care of the maid, who serenely combs her hair out on the porch, and he goes out to the back patio, to sit down with a book underneath the trees, and to wait for Garay López to arrive, but dusk, nightfall, night and midnight follow one upon the other and Garay

López does not appear. Smoking a cigar beneath the full moon, with his inevitable glass of cognac in his hand, chasing away from time to time the clouds of mosquitoes that don't even go away when he waves his hand up close to his face, after having seen Gina to bed, Bianco thinks: "It wasn't him. Perhaps he committed suicide in Buenos Aires, when he received the letter, and what I saw in the doorway was his ghost. Perhaps I had a vision. Perhaps he didn't receive the letter. Perhaps he received it and since he's not the one who fathered what Gina has in her belly, he doesn't deem it imperative to come. Normally, the last of these would be the best hypothesis. With one slight drawback however: if he's not the one who got her pregnant, that means I'm going mad."

But the next morning, Garay López comes to visit them. When the maid announces him and he goes out to the patio to receive him, it is hard for Bianco to recognize him, and as he walks toward him with his hand outstretched, he sees the same figure as the day before, somebody who closely resembles Garay López, who is really almost identical to him, except for the fact that when he comes toward him now with his hand outstretched he looks twenty years older, is wearing a jacket and trousers that are wrinkled and dirty, and has a red, slightly puffy face and not the usual pallor of the Garay López he knows.

"Cher ami."

"Caro dottore," Bianco says, shaking hands with him. On approaching Garay López, a fetid smell reaches Bianco's nostrils, a strong odor of damp straw, slightly rotted, and Bianco notes that even Garay López's eyelids have turned red, and some little red spots also discolor the pupils of his eyes. Contrary to his habit, Garay López immediately lets go of Bianco's hand and when he sees Gina in the distance, sitting in the shade of the porch, he raises his arms with his usual effusiveness, a bit more indolently than is his habit perhaps, and walks over toward her.

Despite Garay López's ostentatious gesture to demonstrate how eager he is to greet Gina, Bianco can follow him across the patio without difficulty, for Garay López's movements are laborious and somewhat clumsy, as though they were executed not by a body made of bones and flexible muscles, but by a rag doll that gets out of joint with every step. Bianco notes that, despite his effusiveness, Garay López stops two or three yards away from Gina, without holding out his hands to her, as is his habit.

"Gina! Gina! Such beauty! A queen! A madonna! And I can appreciate that, because when I was only this tall, they took mine away from me and never gave her back to me," Garay López says, in Italian, with his usual excessive and melodramatic gestures that this time he appears to perform thanks to extraordinary measures that make him tremble and make the skin of his face and his hands redder still. And then, going on in Spanish: "My sister, who saw you in the street one day, wrote me two or three months ago to give me the news. It would have pleased me more to learn of it from the two of you."

The brick-colored eyebrows frown a little.

"What's that you say? Didn't you receive my letter?"

"I've received a number of letters from you since the month of August, cher ami, but they were all business letters," Garay López says. "The only thing you wrote about was wire, turnbuckle, wrenches. Not even a word about your damned positivists."

"I wrote you a week ago to announce that the birth would be taking place at any moment."

"You didn't say a word to me about it," Gina says.

"Unfortunately," Garay López says, "I didn't receive it."

And his face clouds over. "He's lying," Bianco thinks. Looking around him as though he were searching for something, a chair perhaps, Garay López takes two weary steps and leans against the wall. A forced smile makes its way into his reddened eyes.

"Your letter and I must have crossed as I was on my way here," Garay López says. And after his fleeting smile, more a mere hint than a full-fledged glow, his expression clouds over once again.

"I find you a bit tired," Bianco says.

"I do too," Gina says, with a rather indifferent air that strikes Bianco as simulated or shocking.

"A long journey. On horseback," Garay López says. "Since I've had news that the first shipments of wire have arrived, it seemed to me that I ought to be here. I want to convince Papa of the efficacy of the method. But my brother, naturally, took off for the countryside as soon as he saw me arrive."

"He's lying," Bianco thinks. "He's lying, and from the way he's looking at us he's afraid we don't believe him."

"Pretexts," Gina says unexpectedly. "Isn't it, rather, on account of some young lady?"

"A young lady," Garay López repeats, as if he hadn't heard clearly, out of distraction or stunned surprise, and moving a little so as to find exactly the right position and properly perform the movement he is about to make, allows himself to slowly slide down the wall and sit down on the ground.

"Antonio," Gina says.

An expression of unutterable anguish appears on Garay López's face. The polite formulas he offers seem to come from an infinite distance.

"I'm so sorry. Excuse me. Exhaustion. A slight fever, no doubt," he says. And leaning his head against the wall, he fixes his eyes on the rectangle of hazy blue sky outlined above the patio. "What peculiar weather."

"I'll bring you a cognac," Bianco says, and heads hurriedly toward the living room. He fills a glass full of cognac and turns around quickly, so as to return to the patio, but as he is about to leave the room he hesitates a moment, and halting behind the door, which has remained ajar, he spies on the patio through the opening. Gina, sitting in her armchair, waves her hand in front of her face to give herself a little air, or to chase away the mosquitoes that, since early this morning, appear to covet her warm blood and flit about the porch and the patio in clouds that become visible, like a silvery dust, when they pass through rays of sunlight; and Garay López, sitting on the ground, his back leaning against the wall and his legs stretched out on the mosaic tiles of the porch, who slowly shakes his head, as though he were answering, in a discreet or covert way, something that Gina may have said to him just as he, Bianco, was pouring the cognac. Perhaps right now, Bianco thinks, they're communicating in some secret way, without moving their lips, or with their thoughts, perhaps without words, feeling there pass through them, in minute shivers but ones that at the same time they feel, that adverse force that inhabits them and from which he, Bianco, through a great effort of will, has succeeded in excluding himself, knowing none the less that he must remain alert and vigilant. For several seconds too, he experiences, without knowing why, an inexplicable nostalgia for a similar scene, witnessed involuntarily nine months before, when he opened the door of the living room, after having ridden on horseback all afternoon in the rain, and saw them, Gina puffing on a cigar with intense pleasure, Garay López leaning toward her and talking to her in a low voice with a wicked smile on his face. In order to drive away that nostalgia, Bianco opens the door all the way and comes out onto the patio, approaching them and leaning down toward Garay López to hand him the glass of cognac.

"Very kind of you, cher ami," Garay López says, taking the glass so feebly and distractedly that, even if it had been only half full of alcohol, the cognac would have spilled because of the excessive tilt with which, without even realizing it, he is holding the glass.

"What a strange day," Garay López says.

Behind his red eyelids, the red spots in his pupils, his eyes appear to be covered with a very fine film of vapor. He raises the glass to his lips and takes a swallow, but the cognac reappears almost immediately at the corners of his mouth.

"A carriage is waiting for me out in the street," Garay López says. "Would it be too much trouble for you to see me into it, cher ami?"

"You must take care of yourself, Antonio," Gina says. "Who knows what kind of life you lead in Buenos Aires?"

As he slowly gets to his feet, Garay López tries to smile, but the glass falls out of his hand and shatters on the mosaic tiles.

"I don't spare you any of my clumsiness," Garay López says.

"It's nothing," Bianco says. "Come on."

Bianco takes him by the arm and Garay López, before heading for the door, turns toward Gina.

"You are more beautiful than ever. That's the way I prefer you," he says.

"Go get some rest, Antonio," Gina says.

There is an undertone of indifference in her voice, Bianco thinks. She is speaking as if through a transparent veil, as though we were moving in another space, in other eras, as if she alone were part of the present and we were floundering about, disintegrating, in the past. As if she alone existed and we were already prepared to melt away into nothingness. When he obliges Garay López, who seems to refuse at first, to lean against his shoulder so as to accompany him to the street, he smells once more his fetid breath, the smell of damp and rotten straw that he appears to give off, not only from his mouth, but from his entire body. And when they reach the street, Bianco notes, in the face of the servant who is waiting for them at the door, the same bright pink tone that he saw yesterday in Garay López's face on surprising him in the doorway of his house, the bright pink that today has turned crimson, as though the master were preceding the servant in a strange and irreparable process of transformation.

And that same bright red is visible the next day in the face of Garay López's sister, who receives Bianco in the doorway, without asking him in, telling him that Garay López is in bed, with a high fever, and cannot receive him. As she speaks, Bianco observes her reddish eyelids, her eyes clearly outlined in red, as though she had accented them with a red pencil, and the skin of her eyelids reminds Bianco of the times that he has examined his own hand when he has put it in front of a candle flame and looked through it. "It's the sun of these abnormal days that is giving them that color," Bianco thinks, when he is again alone on the sidewalk, and raising his head he looks apprehensively at the hazy sky, and then at the trees whose foliage is being invaded day after day by dark red, yellow and brown. And he is more and more convinced, since on the way home, every so often his path crosses that of somebody whose skin has the same bright pink or red color as Garay López's. It is as if the same changes of color that are contaminating the light of the sun, the horizon and the foliage, were taking place on the human skin, as if the world and the capricious substances which, combining with each other, compose it, were changing because of some unexpected disorder, or obeying some archaic instruction inscribed in their essence and too remote in time for men to be able to foresee it, had decided to give it a bizarre appearance, so as to vary the perpetual green of the trees and the monotonous blue of the sky. He is so thoroughly convinced of this that when he arrives home he goes directly to the bedroom and looks at himself for a long time in the mirror over the washbasin: but it is still the same, the same hair curled in brick-colored waves which his ride on horseback has rumpled a little, but which are rigid enough and so matted together with sweat as to remain more or less tidy, the same white skin, crisscrossed by very fine wrinkles which are accentuated around his eyes, making the dark blue circles under them, the skin that the sun of the pampas neither manages to tan or even to change slightly in color, as if of the entire universe in the process of transformation, he were the last impregnable redoubt, all in one piece, he who has gone through so many changes of identity, which none the less have not sufficed to dissolve the central clot of shadow that constitutes him.

The next day he goes back to Garay López's, and this time it is the other sister who receives him, with skin colored the same bright pink, telling him that Garay López has a fever, and that there are people in the house who are sick, so that Bianco turns away thinking: "All that is a maneuver to gain time, he has me denied entry by his sisters who, because of the strong sunlight, are a little redder than usual." But as he heads north along the river on horseback, he is struck by the intolerable idea that Garay López is really sick and is taking his secret to the grave with him. Because from her, Bianco says to himself, from her I will never learn the truth. She herself probably no longer remembers if anything happened, to the point that if I were to torture her to force her to confess she wouldn't even know what I was talking about, because I now realize where my terror is coming from: she is not inhabited by a force but is that force itself, just as she is as one with what her inner organs ask of her and can be at the same time the mare and the horse when they couple.

"Were you able to see him?" Gina asks from the porch, when she sees him come in.

"No. I saw his other sister," Bianco says, gently brushing her cheek with his lips, but without daring to meet her gaze.

Gina is filing her nails, so she doesn't look at him either. In the silence of the patio, the sound of the file against the edge of her fingernail produces a rhythmical screech that Bianco perceives in an exaggeratedly intense, almost singular way, as though his auditory sensibility were exacerbated.

"And what did she tell you?" Gina asks, filing her nails without raising her eyes.

"He has a high fever," Bianco says. "They say he may not get through the night."

"Poor Antonio," Gina says, without ceasing to file her fingernails.

Bianco shuts himself up in his study. He seems to perceive in Gina something definitively closed, buried beneath layers and layers of a substance at once impalpable and indestructible, sealed several times over, enveloped in tenacious folds, and then again locked up with a number of turns of the key, and in order to make certain that no one, not even herself, will have access to what lies buried, Gina has perhaps thrown the key to the bottom of a dark swamp of forgetfulness. He is sure to see it written in the white abyss of the ceiling. But on the following morning, along with the third or fourth maté that she brings him in the study, the maid hands him a sealed envelope. Bianco finishes the maté, gives the gourd back to the maid, and when he sees her disappear onto the porch, he slowly opens the envelope. Garay López's unmistakable handwriting, a little more shaky than usual, causes him to sit down in his armchair, with relief, to read the note, which is written in French: "Cher ami: this morning I am experiencing an undeniable improvement. But since I know the symptoms of my illness, I greatly fear that it is merely temporary. An abominable crime is weighing on my conscience. Out of respect for your person, from whom I have learned so much, I would not want to go to my grave without confessing it to you. I beg you to come by to see me as soon as you receive this missive."

With an expression of triumph, of sorrow, of relief, of hatred, of bitterness, Bianco crumples the letter and tosses it onto the desk. Ten minutes later, he is galloping southward. The earth is whitish, soft, damp beneath his horse's hoofs; the grass, the trees have an indefinite color, full of different shades that go from a grayish green to a dark brown, a range that passes through blood red, yellow, beige, mahogany. Around the trees, the ground is covered with dead leaves, and the grass that borders the ditches is rotting from contact with the stagnant water, immobilized on the surface by a sort of creamy, furrowed, greenish foam. When he arrives at Garay López's, Bianco dismounts in one leap from his horse, panting and sweating, and when he knocks, he grows impatient when he fails to receive an immediate answer, but as he is on the point of knocking for the second time, the door slowly opens and Garay López himself, dressed with his usual elegance, appears in the doorway.

"Thanks for coming," he murmurs in French.

"Caro dottore, how could I have done otherwise?" Bianco replies, following Garay López through the entry hall.

"There are lots of sick people in the house," Garay López says in a low voice.

They sit down in the living room, facing each other, and Bianco observes that, anticipating his arrival, Garay López has got out a bottle of cognac and two glasses. Without even consulting him, he pours the cognac in the glasses, and after handing one to Bianco, takes the other for himself and leans back in his armchair. Bianco observes him attentively, and Garay López, aware of the look with which Bianco is scrutinizing him minutely allows him to do so with a wan smile. Bianco notes that the red of Garay López's skin has been transformed into a vague color, a yellowish violet, and underneath this indefinable coloring, in the region just below his skin, an infinite number of red spots, like mosquito bites, or like hives, covers all the visible parts of his body.

"Yellow fever," Garay López says when he notes that Bianco has finished inspecting him. Bianco downs a cognac, and looks at him. Garay López's face is also slightly swollen, and the red color, which has disappeared from his face and spread over his entire skin, has none the less remained concentrated in the pupils of his eyes.

"I apologize for the other morning, when you came by on horseback," Garay López says. "I was too ashamed to come meet you face to face."

"You made me have my doubts. I finally decided that it wasn't you," Bianco says. The nape of his neck and his back, between his shoulder blades, are beginning to pound, and perhaps because of the cognac, his shirt is clinging to his skin. "He's about to tell me," he thinks. "He's about to tell me."

"If I hid myself, it was out of respect for your person," Garay López says.

"I believe you," Bianco says.

Garay López falls silent, and drinks a sip of cognac, ceasing to look him straight in the eye, so that Bianco feels a little disoriented. "Perhaps he thinks I already know it through Gina and considers that he's already told me, that along with what he's just said that suffices, so that I'll never know if they were the ones who disordered the bed, who flattened the cushion that afternoon, as I galloped in the rain." Garay López appears to be lost in thought, and when he raises his head and looks at him again, hope is reborn in Bianco's eyes.

"I know that there are obscure things in your life, cher ami," Garay López says. "Terrible ones perhaps. But I've accepted you as you are, without being concerned about your past, in exchange for your friendship. And today we're business partners and friends. I hope that you too can accept me as I am."

"You can count on me," Bianco says. "He believes he's now said everything," he thinks, but he sees that Garay López is covering his face with his free hand and hears him say, between sobs:

"What I must confess to you is abominable. Abominable."

"Calm yourself," Bianco says, downing another cognac and feeling the pounding in the nape of his neck and his back accelerating.

"Last week," Garay López says, more or less controlling his weeping, "I was on duty at the hospital, and I realized that two of the patients had yellow fever. The other doctors had diagnosed their illness as a benign fever. I fell into a panic. I said nothing. And maintaining that my father was very sick, I asked to go on leave, and I came up here, out of fear of becoming infected."

"So that was it. That's your horrendous crime," Bianco says, in a frigid, indignant, reproving tone of voice, beginning to rise to his feet, and thinking: "He's changed his mind at the last minute, he doesn't dare, and he's telling me another one of his stories so that I'll believe that that's the reason why he summoned me."

"But that's not the worst part," Garay López says. "The worst part is that I've brought it with me, I've brought the epidemic with me. My whole family is dying. The servants too. The neighbors are falling fatally ill. The entire city is contaminated."

"That's not true," Bianco says. "That's not true. You're lying."

"Take Gina out to the country. Take her far away."

"You're lying so as to hide something even more horrible," Bianco says.

"Even more horrible?" Garay López says, but Bianco is already at the door of the room and is beginning to stride hurriedly through the entry hall to the front door.

"Take Gina away. Take her away to the country," he can still hear Garay López telling him as he reaches the street. The grayish haze that covers the horizon and the sky give the impression that it is clouding over but the grayish sun is shining down, brightly, intensely, with intermittent ashen beams.

"How is Antonio?" Gina asks, sitting in her armchair on the porch, as she sees him come in.

"He's delirious," Bianco says.

Bianco passes by her almost without halting, barely brushing her cheeks with his lips, and heads off toward the back patio. A sort of fury has come over him at Garay López's, an ill-defined rage whose object at times is Gina, at times Garay López, and at times the very indecision that arouses it, as though it exasperated him to depend on others to verify from outside his palpitations and his intuitions. What is certain is that at siesta-time he fruitlessly fritters away a good while meticulously going over his doubts and hesitations regarding the reasons that might have impelled Garay López to tell him that story of the epidemic, without it ever once crossing his mind that what Garay López has told him, far from being a story, as he refers to it mentally, might have a certain element of truth in it. But Garay López's confession, though Bianco takes no note of it whatsoever in his conception of things, lends a slight tinge of uncertainty to his innermost thoughts, for the day goes by for him in a climate of restless excitement and anxiety. Around five o'clock, Gina gets up from her siesta, looking a bit disoriented and rather flushed, and Bianco, who is watching her from a distance, as though he feared coming into contact with her, and did not feel capable of judging at what precise spatial or emotional point her proximity might begin to become really dangerous, hears her say from the other end of the porch:

"All this upsets you, I realize. How quickly bottles have been getting emptied in these last few months."

With an enigmatic smile, Bianco shrugs, neither acknowledging nor denying her statement. Pretending to read, he retreats behind a book, in the back patio, and allows himself to be enveloped, worried and disconsolate, by the twilight that descends abruptly, focusing particularly on the shriveled foliage. He has vacillated so much that the entire universe seems to vacillate too when darkness finally falls, amid the buzzing of mosquitoes and the sounds and the voices of the maids bustling about in the kitchen or on the patio, preparing dinner or setting the table on the porch, familiar sounds to which, even without paying attention to them, he distractedly attributes a supplementary fragility because of a nameless imminence that seems to be threatening them. During dinner, they scarcely speak of Garay López, and Bianco needs to make a real effort to perceive in Gina anything deliberate about her almost complete silence on the subject. Perhaps she is dissembling so well that she doesn't even give the impression of dissembling, he thinks to himself with a little smile, brief and slightly self-pitying, whereby he admits to himself, not without bitterness, his definite inability to penetrate what lies hidden in her. Almost immediately after finishing dinner, he insists that she go to bed, since he feels her to be so distant when they are together that he needs, paradoxically, to keep her at a distance in order to try to unravel the mystery of her. Toward midnight, wandering about the patios, preceded by the burning tip of the cigar clenched between his teeth, which glows more brightly with each puff, in the darkness of the house, of the entire city perhaps, he realizes that the possibility of knowing is escaping him, slipping away down the endless corridor of the past toward the inconceivable place where frustrated hopes and secrets rust, disintegrate and are reduced to dust. When he goes into the bedroom, Gina, who is sleeping on her back, is emitting short, irregular, intermittent snores, and Bianco lies down at her side and begins to listen to them, as from time to time they decorate her calm breathing like seams of sound reinforcing a delicate thread of breath. Others would have drowned out that breathing, he thinks, with a brusque shake they would have put an end to that sound causing a commotion behind her forehead, without realizing that it is the only proof that something has really taken place. Four or five times, without getting undressed, he lies down alongside her, then gets up again to wander all through the dark house, the porches, the patios, the various rooms, until, beneath the quadrilateral of the front patio the reddish phosphorescence of dawn begins to flow, and he decides to go off to bed to sleep for a couple of hours, waking with a start again and again and telling himself, between the more and more rapid and rather absurd associations of insomnia, that he will get the truth out of Garay López the next day, even if he must use force in order to do so.

But when he goes to see him the next day, he is met by two male nurses at the door, who keep him from coming in. One of them already has a bright pink face which, to tell the truth, gives him a rather healthy look, but on looking into his eyes Bianco perceives the pupils streaked with blood-red filaments. Just as he is about to turn back, telling himself that he will try again later on, a doctor comes out of the house: since he is the same one who is looking after Gina while she is pregnant, Bianco intercepts him on the sidewalk.

"They're all dying in there," the doctor says. "Why do you want to go in?"

"He's my best friend," Bianco says. "I've been with him every day."

"Think of your wife," the doctor says. "You must get her out of the city."

"Let me go in and I promise you to take her to the country this very day," Bianco says. "I've been with him every day. He would already have infected me."

The doctor observes his white skin with close professional scrutiny. And he turns to the nurses.

"Let him go in," he says to Bianco. "I don't know why you're insisting if he's not even going to recognize you."

Before Bianco disappears inside the house, the doctor grabs him familiarly by the sleeve and holds him back for a moment:

"From here you're to go straight to the country," he says.

"I promise," Bianco says.

The house is in such deep silence that, when he comes out of the entry hall onto the first patio, Bianco stops; in the middle of the patio, under the wisteria vine, an old mestiza is sitting in a wicker armchair smoking a pipe, and although she stirs slightly, more indifferent than curious on seeing him appear, Bianco has the impression that her movements are traced in a world where there is no sound, a submarine or sidereal world, where the ashen light is a corporeal medium, a sort of gelatin in which, as in a wax mold, each one of the phases of the old woman's movements are inscribed for a short while, as they echo for a fraction of a second. Bianco halts in the middle of the patio.

"Antonio," he says.

Before making the slightest gesture, the old woman exhales a mouthful of smoke, with the pipe firmly gripped between her teeth, and the little grayish cloud is lost from sight in the gray air, not as though it dispersed in it, but as though the air were a porous substance that had absorbed it. Motioning with her head, the old woman points out one of the doors that open onto the porch. When he pushes it open and goes inside the room, the odor is so strong that Bianco takes out a handkerchief and covers his mouth and his nose. Garay López is lying stretched out on the bed, bare naked, without a pillow, motionless, his wide open eyes fixed on the ceiling, and aside from his coal-black hair and beard and the coal-black hair of his pubis, his whole body is a saffron yellow color, and because he is drenched with sweat, his skin glistens against the soaking wet sheets. He has not only the odor, but also the color of rotting straw, Bianco thinks, and keeping his distance, he leans forward just a little toward him.

"Caro dottore," he whispers.

When Bianco's voice resounds in the room plunged into semidarkness, Garay López's eyelids flutter slightly.

"He deprived me of a mother when he was born," Garay López says.

"Caro dottore," Bianco says. "What Gina has in her belly..."

"He deprived me of a mother," Garay López says.

Bianco notes that he has two small pieces of cotton stopping up his ears, and the soles of his feet have a slightly bluish tinge underneath the uniform yellow of his skin.

"These are your last moments," Bianco says. "Tell me. It has to be you. I won't be able to get anything out of her."

"He deprived me of a mother," Garay López says.

Beneath the white handkerchief with which he is protecting his nose and mouth, Bianco feels his bitter lips contract a little. He is about to lean down closer to the bed, but prudence holds him back. His eyes begin to search the room, until he discovers a cane with a silver pommel, leaning against the side of the chest of drawers. Bianco takes it, and with the tip of it, gives Garay López a few light little taps on the thigh.

"Caro dottore," he says.

Garay López does not move, his wide open eyes fixed on the ceiling, his yellow, lustrous skin that is secreting that odor of rotting straw, his body stark naked, as though made of inorganic material, in which only the eyes, although blurred, still seem alive. The tip of the cane mounts along his body and sinks into his beard, at the level of his cheek.

"Don't pretend," Bianco says. "I saw the unmade bed. I saw the cushion. I saw Gina's face as she puffed on the cigar."

Garay López remains motionless. With the tip of the cane, Bianco gives him two or three light little taps on the cheek, but

Garay López's head offers a strange resistance, as though the muscles of his neck, already rigid, were no longer able to allow him to make the slightest movement. A little trickle of blood begins to run out of one of his nostrils. In fury, Bianco raises the cane, as though he were about to let it lash out at Garay López's head, not of hatred toward him but toward that autonomous blood, toward that yellow substance coloring his body, indifferent to his intentions, that material conspiracy malevolently opposed to his desires, interrupting them, letting them float in the air, making them retreat and pile up in a disorderly heap once more in the black pit where they are born, transforming them into doubt, into suffering, into delirium, toward the universe that seems to become entirely exterior, an immense though absurd structure of which all the fragments are contaminated, becoming active in absurd and momentary combinations that self-destruct at the very instant in which they are formed, toward the incessant sputtering sparks that are now snatching away from him the elongated yellow body and the secrets it contains. Bianco slowly lowers the cane and lets it fall to the floor. When the silver pommel hits the wooden floor, Garay López gives a little shiver.

"He deprived me of a mother when he was born," he says.

Bianco leaves the room. An odor of rotten straw floats all through the house, most likely all through the city. The old woman, sitting under the wisteria vine that has already lost all its leaves, receives on her face the gray shadows of the branches and of the bare, twisted trunks, and does not even raise her head when Bianco, without bidding her goodbye, crosses the patio, goes through the entry hall, and comes out on the street. In the city, the bright pink, red, yellowish faces stand out from the others, pale and anxious, or those of the dark, humble people for whom the epidemic is just one more annoyance under the incomprehensible, disdainful, ash-colored sun. On one corner, a man, leaning with one hand against an adobe wall, is vomiting on the sidewalk, bent double and waving his free hand in the direction of nobody in particular, but simply to show that he is suffering. Another one, a little farther on, leans out a window, and Bianco notes on his face the indefinite color that appeared in Garay López's face, when the red had disappeared and the yellow was not yet dominant. A woman rushes out of a house, screaming and pointing toward the inside to attract the attention of passersby who hurry on. One family is hastily loading things into their cart. On the sidewalk opposite, two policemen are sealing up a door by pasting diagonally across it a wide strip of paper that covers the door handle and the lock. On another corner, the doctor, who is talking with an Army officer, recognizes him and makes a sign in his direction that Bianco interprets as an exhortation to him to leave the city immediately. As he is beginning to leave the downtown district behind, Bianco gives his horse two or three lashes with the reins to hurry him up, but almost immediately thereafter he reins him in a little to have a look at a man who is in his death throes at the edge of a drain. "Yes, yes, he brought the epidemic," Bianco thinks, galloping again, "but he didn't flee out of fear; I myself see all these people around me who are turning red and yellow, and I'm not afraid; he brought it because he received the letter and wanted to see the color of the hair of what is going to come out from between Gina's legs." An incongruous, vaguely demented pride makes him prick up his ears and his eyes sparkle when he notes that even if the entire universe were to collapse, and the sun, the trees, the earth, human beings seem to be already announcing the imminence of this, if it were to shake on its rusty hinges before exploding, his belief would remain unshakable, nor would he cease to keep close watch on the deceptive simulacrum that the adverse whole is unfolding before his eyes with the aim of distracting him and making him lose his way in its swampy jungle. But when he arrives home, and sees Gina sitting in her armchair on the porch, the presentiment of what lies buried in her, out of his reach, in the center of a labyrinth of experience, of blood and of memory, perhaps without Gina herself even knowing it, it is he who wavers, he who might collapse if that archaic thing decanted into Gina's body should decide to emit its deadly radiations.

And they take off for the pampas. Bianco insists that Gina take along her armchair, the only one in which she is really comfortable, and therefore they load a cart with food, bedcovers, water, cognac, and Gina, sitting in the middle of the cart in her armchair, reassures Bianco when, holding the reins, at each jolt he turns around anxiously to ask her if she hasn't hurt herself, if she's comfortable, if she doesn't want them to stop for a while to rest. Leaving the city, they are forced to follow a caravan of carts, horses, people on foot who are fleeing from the epidemic, but once on the outskirts of town, the groups scatter across the pampas and are lost from sight on the anemic and faded horizon, mingling little by little with the tawny grass and the ashen sky. Suddenly they are by themselves in the open countryside, and the cart, drawn by four oxen, makes such slow progress despite the insistent thrusts with the prod with which Bianco goads them, that a person would say that, in a laborious and scarcely efficient way, someone keeps continually pushing the entire landscape backwards, making the oxen and the cart shudder with each jolt, as though they were glued to the tawny-colored carpet that has taken the place of the ground, so that the two of them only reach the cabin at dawn the next day. And, since Gina has slept almost all night long despite the jerks and jolts, it is Bianco who, when he gets down out of the cart, still sees the sky and the horizon judder before his eyes for at least a minute, as though he were still moving along. But they rest all day and sleep all night long, and the next day the two of them awaken in excellent spirits.

"If we stay too long, it may be born here," Bianco says as they are having breakfast.

"What difference does it make?" Gina says. "We have everything that's needed."

"And what if there's a complication?" Bianco asks.

"What complication? There isn't going to be any complication," Gina answers.

"I'm thinking of Antonio. Poor Antonio," Bianco says.

Gina doesn't reply, as though she hadn't heard. Bianco goes outside the cabin. On the pampas nothing is moving, there is not a bird, an animal, a cloud in sight, there is no breeze blowing, and the tawny grass that is so soft that it collects in compact clumps beneath Bianco's boots has no sheen in the unreal, ashen light. "I'm dreaming," Bianco thinks. "I'm doubtless in my house in Paris, fast asleep next to one of my mistresses, after a ball at the embassy, at which I probably drank a little too much champagne, and I've begun to dream, with incoherent fragments of images, that I had a run-in with the positivists, that I went off to Normandy, to Sicily, that I secured a land grant on the pampas, at the end of the world, that I met a doctor named Garay López, and a woman whose name is Gina, that I married her, that there is a hostile force that for obscure reasons is seeking to destroy me, that there's an epidemic in a city and that I am now in an empty space, gray and beige, in which nothing is happening, apart from the silence characteristic of dreams, of the dream of someone who is myself and who does not know that he is sleeping in his bed, in a place called Paris, called the world." But Gina's voice, coming from inside the cabin, brings him out of his dream state.

During the first six days nothing happens, except for the gray sun that slowly crosses the gray sky, the absence of sounds, of a breeze, of anything alive on the pampas, apart from the two of them who rest, read, wait. Finally, on the seventh day, the gray sky begins to turn black, the ashen haze to turn into clouds on the horizon that appear to come up out of the ground, and that, emerging from the line where sky and earth come together, gradually grow bigger and thicker as they move farther away from it, dense clouds with blackish streaks, which pile up to the point that they form a low sky, a dark ceiling, while the entire circle of the horizon is illuminated by flashes of lightning and a line of thunderclaps, like a galloping far in the distance, keeps coming closer and closer. Around noon, it is so dark that they must light an oil lamp in the cabin, as though night had descended, and when the rain begins to fall, for approximately an hour, the air grows darker still and the lightning and the thunderclaps are concentrated just above the cabin, assailing it with intense and intermittent flashes of light, and with vibrations and tremors, until, almost without transition, and giving the impression that the storm had made the afternoon vanish, night falls. The rain is so heavy, so continuous, so persistent, that only the claps of thunder introduce a certain diversity into the monotonous sound of the water, so loud that they must shout to each other to be heard and repeat to each other more than once the sentences that they exchange. Bianco scarcely has time to sleep, keeping watch on the gutters, the electrical discharges, the oil lamps, and casting frequent worried glances at Gina who, sleeping face up on the cot, untouched by the chaos of the storm, with her eyes closed, her enormous belly making the bedcovers curve upward, lies peacefully breathing. And the next morning, standing in the doorway of the cabin, bundled up in a wool jacket, Bianco looks out at the heavy rain that since noon the day before has never once stopped falling. The flashes of lightning and the thunderclaps have become less noticeable, more remote, farther apart. A greenish light, which is neither semidarkness nor bright daylight spreads out in more and more compact folds moving farther off in space, and there is no sky, or earth, or horizons, nothing, only that greenish, uniform medium in which the cabin seems to be floating or to have been deposited, as at the bottom of a fish bowl.

"Autumn has really arrived now," Bianco murmurs in Italian.

The rain little by little turns into a drizzle, until it finally stops altogether at midnight, and the wind, which is beginning to scour the air and the sky, blows heavily during the late hours of the night, until at dawn it stops, so that at first light Bianco sees the reddish rays of sunlight filter in through the cracks in the cabin. At breakfast time they take the table outside and eat in the warmth of the sun.

"The cold is going to put an end to the epidemic," Bianco says.

"Oh, yes, the epidemic," Gina says. And holding her fork suspended halfway to her mouth, she raises her chin slightly toward a point of the pampas at Bianco's back and says: "Somebody's coming."

Bianco turns around. The seven or eight horsemen are so close that he wonders how Gina could have missed seeing them before, unless, instead of coming over the horizon, they have suddenly emerged from where they are now trotting toward the cabin. Bianco pushes apart the two flaps of his jacket so that his revolver is clearly visible at his waist, even though he knows, by the calm trot with which they are approaching, that they are not Indians. As they advance, increasing in size, the details of their attire, their height, their color, gradually become clearer in the transparent air, purified by the rain, rather white in the full light, which also fades the color of the sky, the vast celestial surface in which not a single cloud can be seen. And when he sees that the horseman in the middle, who is riding on a little ahead, is shorter than the other six, three on each side of him, who are perhaps reining in their horses a little so that he will stand out slightly from the group, Bianco recognizes them: "It's the brother. The arsonist. The one who killed his own mother to make a place for himself in the world."

"It's Antonio's brother," he says to Gina in Italian.

The horsemen arrive within a few meters of the cabin, halt, and Bianco goes out to meet them.

"If you care to share our meal," he says, pointing to the table with a vague gesture.

"We've already eaten," the brother says, thin as a rail as he sits hunched over his horse, but tense, muscular, still with the face of a child, just a little less ragged than the brawny gauchos, more heavyset and older than he, who would slit the throats of an entire town or would allow their own throats to be slit if he asked them to. The sombrero does not succeed in hiding a few white spots that doubtless descend from the crown of his head to the upper part of his forehead, abnormally bald for his age. His curt, somewhat shrill, rapid voice has expressed neither enmity nor disdain, but simply haste to broach the subject that has brought him here. Bianco notices this.

"What brings you here?" he says, feeling that after weeks, months, during which his pragmatic instinct has been buried underneath dense and sticky layers of unknown and fearful emotions, the right side of his personality, that almost indolent facility with which he is capable of reigning over everything having to do with the practical, that secretly he despises, is beginning to emerge again, intact and natural, like a great artist who has begun to set down his first self-assured brush strokes after a long illness.

"I've lost my whole family," the other says.

"We know," Bianco says. "Our most sincere condolences. We too have lost a very dear friend."

The brother says nothing.

"Why don't you dismount?" Bianco says. "I suppose that

you've come to talk to me about the commercial enterprise that I created with your brother. The death of your father, doubtless, confronts you with a dilemma."

A surprised expression appears on the brother's face on noting that Bianco has so easily guessed the reason for his visit.

"Dismount," Bianco says. "A glass of cognac will make our ideas clearer."

After hesitating briefly, the brother passes the reins of his mount to the gaucho who is next to him and climbs down off his horse. And it is when his feet touch the ground and he begins to walk toward the table that he appears for the first time to notice Gina, sitting in her armchair at the end of the table, observing him openly, but without curiosity, with those frank, direct eyes of hers in which, instead of a definite emotion, obscure, unfathomable undulations blaze, eyes which at first make you turn your gaze away and then, at every moment, raise it uneasily and furtively so as to try to meet once more, fleetingly and fruitlessly, her disturbing gaze. When he comes closer to her, and sees that she is pregnant, about to give birth at any moment, his eyes remain riveted on the belly wedged in between the armchair and the edge of the table, with the same fearful and all-consuming anxiety with which a dog might keep a close eye on the whip that is threatening him. When he comes back with the bottle of cognac, Bianco knows that he has him at his mercy, that the savage animal capable of going out at night to lay claim to the total sovereignty of his desire, to set fire to fields of wheat, has just entered an aura that neutralizes him, disarms him, softens the hardened walls in the moldy caverns within him, and causes them to allow to filter upward into the light of day, like sulfurous vapors, what was hidden inside them beneath layers of disdain and cruelty. Not only, Bianco thinks, is he going to agree to be my business partner, but also my first customer, and from this afternoon on, he will teach those

murderous gauchos to manufacture bricks, and for the first time
in his life he will be able to see a little farther than his absurd
and monomaniacal fixation on cattle, and accept that the thousands and thousands of foreigners who are arriving in the country
can sow a little wheat on the edge of his property, in his own
fields if the occasion arises; and instead of going off stupidly to
burn the harvests, he will finally learn that it is much better to
buy them at a low price, store them in the port in the city, and
sell them on the European market at ten times the price he paid
for them. And all that because he has entered the magic circle,
the magnetic field, the space that lies beneath a spell where
force, magma, promise, the space without a name and without
an ultimate purpose, neither friendly nor unfriendly, which,
with equal indifference, brings us into the light or crushes and
grinds us until we are mingled with the frozen dust of stars.

"As a friend, Antonio was better," Gina says, as the horsemen
ride off across the pampas, "but as a business partner, this one
seems more suitable."

Bianco replies with an amiable grunt. The kindly autumn
sun warms his skull through the abundant curly crop of his
brick-colored hair, and it also warms the cognac; a beam of light
breaks through the surface of the liquid, travels down through
the glass, and projects a luminous spot on the wood of the table.

"I have a surprise for you," Gina says. And putting her hand
in the pocket of her dress she takes out the three rectangular
images with rounded corners, the light blue backs of them identical, and the three very different designs on the face of them:
the walnut, oval and divided into two equal parts by two parallel
vertical lines very close together, light brown on a white background, which contains, in each one of its two halves, several
sinuous furrows that resemble the brain's, the bright yellow
banana that is printed diagonally against a pink background,
and the bunch of grapes that is no more than of a series of little

circles of a blue-violet hue, forming several irregular rows, each made up of a lesser number of circles, an inverted triangle, against a bright red background which gives the primitively drawn bunch of grapes a third dimension.

"Do you think this is the right time?" Bianco says.

"We haven't tried it for months," Gina answers. "It's time to begin again now."

"I don't know if I'm able to concentrate," Bianco says.

"Let's try," Gina says.

Without haste, if not to say without conviction, without illusions perhaps as to the reality of his former powers, or perhaps as to their present efficacity, and even their pertinence, Bianco rises to his feet and stands alongside the table for a moment, hesitating, contemplating the three images that Gina has in her hand. After a few seconds, without saying a word, he slowly begins walking toward the cabin. When he goes inside, his eyes blinded by the light outside, he is obliged to grope about in the semidarkness until he finds the wooden bench on which to sit down so as to bring about in the best possible conditions the concentration required by the practice of telepathic transmission. With his arms outstretched, leaning down a little so as to touch the wood of the bench in the semidarkness that is tending to disappear, struggling against the illusion that the result of the experiment will be satisfactory, since, in order to defend himself from the hostile force, in order to escape its aura, he thinks that the most prudent thing to do is not to expect anything, not to desire anything, not to let himself be attracted by the insidious magnet that makes of his entire being a thin thread of defenseless metal moving at top speed, irresistibly, toward the unknown. But when his knees touch the edge of the bench, that very thing against which he wants to struggle makes him forget his intentions. So that he sits down on the bench, and prepared to concentrate, closes his eyes and ceases to move.

Envoi

Those who, perplexed, see the days and the nights go by without any reason, those who drag along from their past a great weight behind them, those who think that every minute to come is the last and that they are not prepared for so much reality, those who believe themselves to be the black stain, the dregs of the world, those who wander about lost on the indifferent crust of their mornings, those who have received only waiting as their inheritance and have nothing else to pass on, those who are dying of hunger, of cold, of sadness, in the muddy vacant lots on the edge of town, those who have made of night their dwelling, of the day their martyrdom, those who know that they are outlaws, frail, unreal, mysterious, were crowded together at the entrance to Waldo's cabin on the outskirts of the city, waiting for the sergeant, who was inside, and who had just promised them that Waldo, as soon as he got up from his afternoon siesta, would be ready to receive them. With a package of sweets that he had bought, following Bianco's advice, the Calabrian circulated among the many people who, in all truth, formed a small crowd. The Calabrian knew many of those who were waiting, since it was the third consecutive day on which they had been trying to be received by Waldo, fruitlessly, since there was such a multitude, because of the epidemic perhaps, that Waldo, even though he began at eight in the morning and stopped at eight at night, was unable to receive them all. Tired of roaming about the pampas, about the cities, yearning to go back to see his family that he had sent back to Italy, without knowing whether to bring them back again or else go back himself to where he had come from, but undecided, superstitious, fearful of the future, overwhelmed by his adversities, the Calabrian had made up his mind to consult Waldo, whose prophecies were said to be infallible, so as to leave his hesitations behind him and face his future with greater certainty. What Waldo told him to do he would do. But it had been three days now that he had been waiting outside in front of the whitewashed cabin with his package of sweets and three banknotes in his pocket, which he had set aside from the money that he had saved for the passage home, without managing to obtain an audience. Finally the sergeant appeared in the doorway, with the empty sleeve of his shirt folded back and fastened down with a safety pin at the right shoulder, and raising his one hand in which he was holding a dead cigar between his index and middle finger, he announced that Waldo was ready to receive them, but that, since there were so many people, instead of individual consultations, he would have them come in by groups, so that nobody would be left outside. The multitude began to crowd around the entrance, showing their gifts, their banknotes, and all of them claimed that they had been waiting for three days, five days, a week, so that the Calabrian, who was of rather short stature but strong and muscular, began to elbow others aside so as to be among the first to get inside. They took a woman out who had had a fainting spell from the commotion, and slipping through those who made way for her to get outside for a breath of air, he managed to get as far as the door and enter with the first group, but not before receiving from someone he had pushed aside a hard blow on the back of the neck. The sergeant tapped them on the shoulder with his one hand and let them come inside, telling them that they should get their gifts and banknotes ready. The Calabrian took out his three bills, folded them lengthwise, and held them in his clenched fist, letting the ends of them stick out so that they were clearly visible. When the fifteen people were inside, they tried to crowd around Waldo, who was sitting in a chair with a straw seat and who appeared to be indifferent to the commotion, but his older sister, the sergeant's wife, stopped them and pushed them back so as to make them keep their distance. Then the sergeant closed the door of the cabin and came to help his wife gather up the bills and the gifts, as La Violadita, dressed in white, leaned toward Waldo and said something to him in his ear. Finally a long, solemn silence fell in the room, and Waldo, who was slowly nodding his head and making his saliva hiss with his teeth, began to give forth from the bottom of his throat a rasping, humid, incomprehensible sound, that little by little transformed itself into an octosyllabic distich, without the Calabrian's knowing that it was either a distich or octosyllabic, which Waldo repeated several times, in a louder voice each time, but with a pronunciation so deformed by his clenched teeth and the hissing saliva that the Calabrian, who was one of those farthest away and who, having spent his seven years on the pampas almost exclusively in the company of other Italians, had almost no command of the language of the country, was unable to understand what they meant. The two or three fragments of words that reached his ears had no more meaning for him than the harsh and guttural sound from which Waldo had formed his prophetic couplets. Finally, Waldo fell silent and remained motionless once again, with a blank expression on his face, turned slightly away from the part of the room where those who had come to consult him were standing, and as the Calabrian hoped that the prophecy would be formulated for a second time to see if he understood any of it, the sergeant and his wife politely but firmly showed them to the door. Hence, the Calabrian, disoriented, found himself standing in the back patio a few seconds later, without having understood the prophecy, without therefore knowing, any more than he did before he entered, what decision to make, and without the banknotes and the sweets.

HIC INCIPIT PESTIS

Founded in 1986, Serpent's Tail publishes the innovative and the challenging.

If you would like to receive a catalogue of our current publications please write to:

FREEPOST
Serpent's Tail
4 Blackstock Mews
LONDON N4 2BR

(No stamp necessary if your letter is posted in the United Kingdom.)